"I want to sell the far

"But why?" Rose asked, in shock.

Jesse ran a hand through his hair. "I can't live here after what I went through with my father. I didn't come back because I *couldn't* come back."

"But you don't have to," she said evenly. "I can run this place. You don't have to step foot on this property ever again."

"You're not hearing me. I've been thinking about it since he passed away last year."

Rose felt like she'd been punched in the gut. "But how could you do that? It's my home and my job."

Jesse shifted uncomfortably. "I'm sorry, but I can't keep something I don't want."

"Wow. Message received." Rose felt all the old hurt feelings rush back. The heartache and sadness after he'd left her. Now that he was back and threatening to sell the place, a new kind of hurt settled in. Not just fear she'd lose her home and job, but fear she'd lose the life she loved.

Would she ever forgive him? Or better yet, would she forgive him again?

Debut author **Stacie Strong** was born and raised in Jacksonville, Florida. She and her husband raised two children, and as empty nesters, now have a soft spot for rescue cats. Stacie worked in corporate America for fifteen years before moving on to education. Currently, she is an academic adviser at Jacksonville University, where her students surprised her with the Wind Beneath My Wings award, honoring her for her dedication to students.

Books by Stacie Strong

Love Inspired

Sunflower Farms Redemption

Visit the Author Profile page at LoveInspired.com.

Sunflower Farms Redemption

STACIE STRONG

LOVE INSPIRED
INSPIRATIONAL ROMANCE

LOVE INSPIRED®

INSPIRATIONAL ROMANCE

Recycling programs
for this product may
not exist in your area.

ISBN-13: 978-1-335-59743-4

Sunflower Farms Redemption

Copyright © 2024 by Stacie Butts

For questions and comments about the quality of this book, please contact us
at CustomerService@Harlequin.com.

® is a trademark of Harlequin Enterprises ULC.

Love Inspired
22 Adelaide St. West, 41st Floor
Toronto, Ontario M5H 4E3, Canada
www.LoveInspired.com

Printed in Lithuania

MIX
Paper | Supporting
responsible forestry
FSC® C021394

But they that wait upon the Lord shall renew their strength; they shall mount up with wings as eagles; they shall run, and not be weary; and they shall walk, and not faint.
—*Isaiah* 40:31

This book is dedicated to my parents,
who supported me in every way.
Thank you, Mom and Dad.

Chapter One

❦

"Are there any volunteers to milk old Betsy here?" Rose McFarland asked the small crowd gathered in the barn for her talk on farm animals. Weekends at Sunflower Farms in sunny Florida were busy, and this Saturday was no different. A number of hands flew up, mostly kids, as the adults stood by and watched. She scanned the room for someone old enough to follow instructions. Her eyes landed on a familiar face in the back. One she hadn't seen in a long time.

Jesse.

His dark eyes held hers for a heartbeat. She was the first to break the contact and glance away.

Rose sucked in her breath as she calmed herself. Everyone was waiting for her to pick a volunteer, not turn to a pile of mush…

Ex-boyfriends had a way of doing that to a girl.

Rose cleared her throat and quickly selected a young boy for the task. She led him to a stool next to Betsy, then explained to the group how to milk a cow. The whole time she spoke, she was aware that Jesse watched her every move. It was hard to concentrate, but somehow, she managed to get through her speech. Whether she rushed through it or spoke clearly, she had no clue. All she could think about was her unexpected guest.

Betsy lowed at the boy's clumsy attempt to milk her. Rose reached down and helped him with his hand placement, giving him more direction until finally he was successful. Milk streamed into the bucket. With a snaggletooth smile, the boy grinned up at Rose.

"You did it. Great job. Just a few more squirts, and we'll let someone else try," Rose said absently. She pushed her long ponytail off her shoulder. Even though she was dressed in a short-sleeved gingham top and shorts, she suddenly felt hot.

When she ushered the boy off the stool, the small audience gave him a round of applause.

"We have time for another volunteer," Rose offered.

Again, many hands went up and a chorus of "Me! Me! Me!" filled the barn.

Rose shot a sugarcoated smile Jesse's way. It only took him a second or two to catch on that he'd just been volunteered. He slowly shook his head.

Rose ignored him, marched through the audience and pulled him up to the front of the group. He wore blue jeans and a polo shirt, and his black hair was shorter than he used to wear it. Somehow, he was more handsome than she remembered. How could that be?

"Hello, sir. What's your name?" Rose asked as she pulled him toward the stool.

"You know my name," he countered. His voice was deeper, more mature. He'd always been more than a head taller than her petite height. That hadn't changed.

He stared down at her, his dark eyes sparkling with amusement.

She lifted her chin. "I think I've forgotten it. It's been so long since I've seen you. Something like ten years, you know." She said it loud enough for the crowd to hear, as if it were all part of the show.

Jesse played along and sat on the stool. "My name is Jesse."

"Ah…that's right. It's Jesse. Well, Jesse, go ahead and try milking Betsy. Or do you need me to show you how first?" she challenged.

"Nah," he drawled. "I think I have it." Jesse expertly milked Betsy, as if he'd milked a thousand cows before. The rhythmic sound of milk hitting the stainless steel bucket filled the room. Jesse glanced up at Rose. "There. How'd I do?"

"Great job. It's like…like you're an old pro," Rose stammered.

Come on, Rose, spit it out, she thought. Maybe it wasn't such a good idea to call Jesse out. Now that he was next to her, it was harder to think.

"I've done my share of milking cows, if you'll recall," he said under his breath, loud enough for only Rose to hear.

Nearby, a little girl begged to try. Rose realized she needed to get on with the talk and send Jesse away. When was the last time a guy had made her this nervous? Reluctantly, Rose said, "Th-thank you so much, Jesse. We'll give the next person a turn."

The crowd clapped when Jesse stood, and he gave a

good-natured bow. Rose rolled her eyes. Really? Why did people always love him?

Jesse waggled his brows at Rose and treated her to a lopsided grin, then took his place in the back once again. Rose's traitorous stomach did a little flip-flop, which was completely irritating. This was the same guy who'd broken her heart once. She shouldn't give him a second thought.

Rose rushed through the rest of her lecture about cows, skipped the chickens and goats portion, and dismissed her small audience early. She had to admit, Jesse's unexpected appearance had rattled her.

A minute to collect herself was necessary. This was the same guy that had left her ten years ago. They'd been young and in love…and he'd just left. How could he do that to her? And now he shows up after all this time and expects her to be excited to see him?

Out of the corner of her eye, she saw Jesse head toward her. She ignored him and abruptly turned to lead Betsy out of the back barn door, toward the corral. Rose wasn't ready to talk to him.

"Wait up," Jesse called. He pushed his way through the crowd and followed her out.

Rose heard him but didn't stop until she reached the corral gate. She swung the door open with a shaky hand, then closed Betsy in. When Rose turned to leave, Jesse was in her path. His broad chest blocked her way.

He smelled clean like fresh soap. She hated that she liked it. Rose tipped her head back to look him in the face. "What are you doing?" she asked, exasperated.

"I'm getting your attention, since you're determined to ignore me."

"I'm not ignoring you. I'd like to point out I let you help milk Betsy. Now, if you will excuse me, I have work to do," she countered, even though he was right; she was totally ignoring him.

"I need to talk to you."

"Now's not a good time. Weekends are our busiest days, and Justin called in sick, so I'm short-staffed." Rose stepped around him and headed back to the barn with a determined step. She let the door close in his face.

Jesse was nothing if not persistent. He opened the door and walked in behind her. "I'm here. Let me help?"

Rose came to an abrupt stop, turned and glared at him. "Now you're offering to help? Where have you been the past year, since your father passed away? And may I ask, where were you when he was sick? You've been gone for ten years."

"I came back for the funeral," he protested.

"Whoopee. You deserve a medal," she said, annoyance obvious in her voice.

"I know you're angry, but you of all people know my history with him."

She knew Jesse had left to get away from his father, but Rose was the casualty of that decision. His leaving broke her heart. Then after his father passed away, he should have come back to help with the farm that he inherited. But he still chose to stay away. She couldn't help that it was a sore subject for her.

Rose shook her head. "I'm not having this conversation right now. I have work to do."

The crowd had mostly dispersed from inside the barn, but there were still a few patrons nearby who openly gaped at them. Jesse pulled Rose to a corner and lowered his voice. "If you're that busy, let me help today."

She really did need the help if she wanted the day to run smoothly. She'd be a fool to let him go. But deep down, she knew she'd be a fool to let him stay.

Finally, she gave in. Putting her hands on her hips, she stared up at him. "Against my better judgment, I will take you up on the offer. That is, if you think you can find your way around. We've made some changes over the years."

"I think I can handle it," he said dryly.

"Fine. You can help. Do you remember how to drive the tractor?"

He let out a low chuckle. "I spent more hours than I'd like to remember on a tractor. I'm sure it will come back to me. Kind of like riding a bike...or milking a cow. Right?"

Rose ignored the joke. "Great," she said. The word came out a little shrill. She cleared her throat. "Justin was supposed to run the hayrides today. It's one of our most popular activities. You can take over for him. Let's get you a schedule, then I'll take you to the tractor."

Again, she left him in her dust as she walked out the front of the barn and threaded her way through the crowd. The gift shop was located on the first floor of the garage, and Jesse followed Rose inside. She noticed him scanning the room. They'd recently redecorated. A large counter with the cash register took up one wall, and the other three were loaded with shelves and souvenirs. The room was painted a cheerful yellow and the black Sunflower Farms sign, that Rose had designed, hung behind the counter.

"This is new," Jesse commented. "I like it. It's very nicely done."

Rose smiled. She hated to admit it, but his praise meant a lot. Even though she hadn't inherited the place like Jesse, she'd put her blood, sweat and tears into it. It was her baby. "Thanks. I'm glad you like it. The visitors park their cars out front and have to walk through the gift shop to pay for their entrance into the farm. Most end up walking back through at the end of the day to purchase something."

"Clever."

"Yes, I thought so." Rose led him to the counter. "Let me introduce you to Lolly. She works in the gift shop."

Lolly's blond head was tilted down as she counted out change for a customer. When the guest left, Lolly smiled at Rose and Jesse. "Hi!" She was always in a good mood, making her the perfect person to greet arriving guests.

"Lolly, this is Jesse. He's Mr. Cooper's son. He owns Sunflower Farms now."

"Nice to meet you." Lolly reached across the counter and shook Jesse's hand. She seemed a little starry-eyed as she gazed up into his handsome face.

"Nice to meet you, as well," Jesse said. He'd always been oblivious to the attention he attracted from the opposite sex.

"I am so sorry about your dad," Lolly offered. "We all miss him terribly. He was a wonderful person."

Jesse shuffled uncomfortably, but to his credit, he didn't get into his difficult relationship with his father. He politely answered, "Thank you."

Rose jumped in. "Jesse has offered to fill in for Justin today with the hayrides. Can you hand him a schedule?"

Lolly pulled out one of the brochures. "Here you go. The first hayride starts in a few minutes, so you may want to head out there."

Jesse perused the brochure. "This is impressive. The farm has come a long way. Are you open to the public every day?"

"Just the weekends. People come out to see the sunflowers and for a glimpse of life on a farm," Rose said.

"I see there are a few other classes this afternoon. Rose, do you give those classes, too?"

"I do, and speaking of which, the gardening class starts soon. We need to get a move on. Let me show you to the tractor you'll be using."

Rose directed Jesse down an out-of-the-way dirt path that led to the warehouse. Her nerves were starting to calm, so she didn't rush ahead but walked next to him.

"You've been gone for a long time," she said finally. "Why did you come home?"

"That's something I want to talk to you about," he said.

She glanced up at him. Even in the bright afternoon light, his eyes were nearly black. She'd always envied him for his long lashes. Rose caught herself and looked away.

"Well, you came at the worst time," she said. "Saturdays are our busiest day."

"Yeah, I see that now. Sorry. I thought it'd be a good time to catch you." He kept his hands tucked in his pockets as they walked.

"You should have called ahead."

"I didn't think about it."

"Well, think about it next time," she chastised. Then immediately berated herself. What was she thinking? The guy owned the place. He was her boss.

But he was also her ex-boyfriend. Didn't that give her the right to call him out?

What was the real reason he'd shown up today? She'd been running everything for years. Even when Mr. Cooper was healthy, she'd taken over management of the farm. As he grew more ill, he'd put her name on the bank accounts and she'd started paying the bills and the salaries. It was almost like the place was hers.

At the warehouse, she checked her watch. They were running behind. "We'll have to talk later. For now, we need to get the hayride going."

The tractor was hooked up to a flatbed trailer covered with fresh hay. Jesse circled the tractor and trailer, examining them. He kicked a tire or two in the process. He picked up a piece of hay, twirled it between two fingers, then stuck the end in his mouth.

It reminded Rose of his dad. She'd seen James Cooper do the same thing countless times. She kept the observation to herself. No doubt Jesse wouldn't appreciate being compared to him.

"I can't remember. Did you guys ever offer hayrides when you lived here as a kid?" Rose asked.

"No, and I'm surprised that you do now. Maybe it's

the firefighter in me, but this doesn't look all that safe."
He tugged at the trailer's tailgate to check its security.

"Firefighter, huh?" she asked.

He looked over at her, "Yeah. Why?"

Rose shrugged. "No reason. Just didn't know that's what you'd ended up doing since you never stayed in touch with me or your dad. Anyway, the hayride is safe enough," she said. "We don't let the kids get on without an adult, and you'll need to drive as slow as the tractor will go."

She entered a security code on the warehouse keypad, reached inside and grabbed the tractor keys. She gave Jesse the code in case he needed to get back in, then instructed him about the hayride route.

As Rose handed Jesse the keys, their hands brushed momentarily. She ignored the goose bumps that went up her arm. Jesse seemed unfazed.

"Thank you. It'll be in good hands, I promise," he said as he jumped up into the seat.

"Better be."

He waggled those eyebrows at her again. "Trust me, you won't be sorry."

She had the uncomfortable feeling she would be *very* sorry. What did his unexpected appearance mean?

He cranked the noisy tractor. "You want a ride?" he offered over the hum of the engine.

"No, thanks. I'll walk back." She watched the tractor and trailer disappear down the dirt path, kicking up a trail of dust.

Time for her gardening class to start. Inhaling deeply and blowing out a steadying breath, she set out on her trek to the main house and garden. It was a long walk back, but her thoughts were consumed by Jesse.

Back when they dated, he was a good guy, and now he was probably quite the catch if he was still single, but Rose had her heart broken by the man once. It had devastated her. So, whatever this visit was about, she'd have to keep her distance. She was sure he'd leave again… maybe for another ten years.

The tractor rumbled along, causing Jesse to bump and sway with each dip of the trail. From the high seat, he stole a parting glimpse of Rose and was reminded of the day he'd left her long ago.

She'd been a skinny eighteen-year-old girl, standing outside her house with tears in her eyes. He'd ended things between them and left, breaking both their hearts.

He hadn't allowed himself to think about that in years. But being back on the farm had created a tidal wave of memories. He'd stayed away from Sunflower Farms because of the bad memories of his mom's death and how his dad treated him after that. Now that he was here, it wasn't his mother or father he was thinking of.

Memories of Rose flooded back. He'd loved her, even if it was only puppy love. He'd always felt guilty for breaking up with her the way he did, so suddenly. One day they were high school sweethearts, the next he was on his way to the University of Kentucky, with no plans to look back. She'd stayed in the small town of Eagletin, Florida, to get her degree in agriculture sciences at the local university, while he had wanted nothing more than to escape from home.

Jesse shook his head to clear it. He needed to pay attention and figure out where he was going. The dirt trail ended, and he found himself in a field behind the main house and barn. The grass was short and dry, as if it hadn't rained in forever.

He followed the signs to the hayride pickup area, passing several picnic tables with families sitting in the cozy October sunshine, eating their lunches. As he passed the garden entrance, he noticed a small crowd was gathered inside. Were they waiting for Rose to give her class on gardening? Since she was on foot, they'd be waiting awhile.

Jesse rolled up to the hayride staging area. A line of people waited behind two brightly colored orange cones. He greeted them and started helping the first group aboard. The flatbed filled up quickly, and he set off on the well-worn path.

They rode through acres and acres of sunflowers, an impressive display of God's beauty in the fall, with its sea of yellow against a powder-blue sky. The blossoms had faces as large as plates and stems as tall as a man.

As Jesse drove them to the citrus grove at the back of the property, he recalled how his parents had planted seedlings when he was a small boy. Now the trees were tall and full of oranges, lemons and limes that would be ready to pick in the next few months.

The last leg of the ride had them going through the strawberry fields, finally ending in a full circle back at the hayride staging area.

By the end of the day, he'd made several trips around the property, and he'd barely seen Rose. When he did spot her, she was busy helping guests or giving classes. After only one day of observing her, he could tell she was the glue that kept the place together. But was it too much to manage by herself with his dad gone?

He'd been surprised to see her lead the talk on the farm animals. The Rose he'd known in high school had always been smart and outgoing, but now she was a self-assured, confident woman.

Later, the last of the guests drove off as the afternoon sun moved lower in the sky. Long shadows ran across the yard, and the warmth of the day was replaced with the cooler air of autumn. Jesse put away the tractor and went in search of Rose. As he walked, the scent of the land brought back vivid memories of his childhood on the farm, both good and bad.

He passed Lolly emptying trash cans near the picnic tables. "Have you seen Rose?" he asked her.

Lolly greeted him with a friendly smile, "You can try the barn. She's probably putting the animals away and feeding them."

"Thanks." Then Jesse thought to add, "Do you need help with the trash?"

Lolly seemed surprised by his offer. "No, I've got this. You go on. Thanks, though."

Nodding, Jesse strolled over to the barn. Two horses had already been put away in their stalls. They hung their elegant necks over the doors, and Jesse paused long enough to pet one of them, a brown horse with a white blaze. It nuzzled Jesse's hand, but nickered when it saw Rose round the corner with a bucket of feed.

"I know what you want, buddy," Jesse said to the horse eyeing the food.

"Try again." Rose pulled up next to him. "She's not a buddy."

Jesse chuckled. "Whoops. Sorry, old girl." He scratched her neck. "What's her name?"

"That's Missy, and over there—" she nodded toward a black horse "—that's Moe."

"They're pretty friendly."

"Yeah, well, like the rest of us, they've gotten used to entertaining the crowds."

Rose opened Moe's stall door, went in and dumped feed in his trough. Missy was next. Jesse stepped back and stayed out of the way. When she came out with the empty bucket, she stopped beside him. "I'm surprised you're still here. I would have thought the hay-ride would have scared you away for another ten years."

"I guess I deserve that." Seemed like she was still angry at him for leaving.

"I'd say you deserve more than that."

"I need to talk to you. It's important," Jesse said.

Rose stood with her shoulders squared and her head held high, like a woman in charge. She tossed her pony-tail over a shoulder. Little wisps escaped and fell loosely around her face. Back in high school, she'd always kept her hair highlighted blond. Now it was her natural shade of light brown. She was prettier than he remembered. In his time away from Eagletin, she'd grown up. He was sorry he wouldn't be here long enough to get to know the woman she'd become.

"It's been a long day, and I need to clean up and get some rest. We have to do it all over again tomorrow," Rose said.

"I know you're busy. Let me help you put things away, then we can talk."

Rose bit her lip as she studied him. "Fine. Did you put the tractor in the warehouse?"

"Of course."

"That's a start. Come on, you can help me with the rest of the animals."

They moved the cow—Betsy, he remembered—into a stall and fed her. Then Jesse followed Rose outside, and together they fed and watered the rest of the animals.

"What do you think of the farm now? Is it different from what you remember?" she asked him.

"It's something else. I'm dumbfounded by the changes. I had no idea I'd find it this way."

She grinned at him. "I know. It's come a long way."

"I can't get over how many visitors were on the grounds today. When I lived here as a kid, we only had the strawberry picking open to the public. We sold the sunflowers to florists, but they were never the main business for the farm," he mused aloud. "A busy Saturday back then meant a dozen or so families would come out to pick strawberries just during the season. Today, I'm sure I saw several hundred people come through. It felt more like an amusement park attraction than a farm at times."

"I can't tell if you think that's good or bad." Rose handed Jesse an armful of hay and led him to the goat pen. He scattered the fresh hay for the goats while she refilled their water troughs. The four goats followed her around bleating until she stopped long enough to pet them.

Jesse watched her give each of them attention. "It's just different from what I remember."

She straightened up and led Jesse out of the pen. "We had to do something. Your dad was going to lose the farm if we didn't figure out another revenue stream. We still sell the sunflowers and citrus, and we have the strawberry picking, too, but there's a market for the farm experience. Petting the animals, learning about agriculture, and most of all, people want to see and pick the sunflowers when they're in season. You have to admit, it's one of the most beautiful things you've ever seen."

"It is. And you've been strategic planting flower fields near the front of the farm where the guests are. Back in the day, we never had this many fields."

"It was a learning process. We've definitely adapted over the years. Next weekend is the fifth annual Sunflower Festival. Now talk about impressive, we'll have twice as many people here for that."

"It's hard to believe this place could be more crowded. I'm surprised my dad let you make changes or have a festival. He was always so set in his ways."

They were headed toward the chicken pen, but Rose stopped and turned to study him. "I know you had a strained relationship with him, and he was the reason you left. But you have to know, he changed."

Jesse shook his head. "It's hard for me to imagine that. You have no idea how awful he was to be around after my mom died."

"I remember. I know you tried to hide it from me when we were dating, but there were times I caught glimpses of it. Especially when I worked weekends here. And then after you left, he needed my help even more. I agree, he was a difficult man to be around back then, but I'm telling you, he changed."

Jesse held up a hand to stop her. "Don't. I didn't come here to talk about him. He doesn't get off that easy."

"Fine. Not today, but one day, you need to hear it. Come on, we're losing sunlight."

They checked on the chickens and filled their water dish. With the coming evening, they had moved to their coop for the night. She shut them in.

Jesse followed Rose back to the gift shop. "Where are you living now?" he asked.

"I'm living on the farm. I moved into the second floor over the gift shop, what used to be the garage years ago. Turned it into a small apartment."

"I'm surprised you didn't move into the main house after my dad passed."

"It never felt right. Truthfully, it belongs to you. It wasn't my place to take over. Besides, my apartment is comfortable."

Lolly walked out of the gift shop and stopped when she saw them approach. "Hey Rose, everything's clean, the day's sales are in the safe, and I restocked the shelves. I'm heading out now. Will I see you at church tomorrow morning?"

"I'll be there. Save me a seat."

"Will do. It was nice meeting you, Jesse. You're welcome to come, too," she offered.

"I thought you all had the farm open to the public tomorrow."

"We do, but it doesn't open until one. So, there's time for church in the morning. Really, you should come. Everyone would love to see you again," Rose said.

"I think I'll pass this time."

"Okay, maybe next time, then. Good night, you two," Lolly said.

They watched her get into her car and drive away, then Rose turned to Jesse. The sun had set, leaving them in the evening twilight. A nearby floodlight sensed their movement and switched on. Fingers of light wrapped around them in the darkness.

"Thank you for helping today," she said. "I'm sorry I couldn't make time for you earlier, but you took me by surprise. So, what was it you wanted to talk about?"

Jesse stuck his hands into his pockets as he picked his words. Perhaps blunt was best.

"I want to sell the farm."

Chapter Two

Rose had to pick her jaw up off the ground.

"Did you say you want to sell the farm? But why?" she asked, in shock. When Jesse had said he needed to talk to her, she hadn't imagined it was to tell her this.

Jesse ran a hand through his hair. It struck her that his face appeared haunted in the shadows from the floodlight. "I can't live here after what I went through. Not after everything."

"But you don't have to come back," she said, trying to keep calm. The man was threatening her livelihood. "I can run this place. I've been doing fine this whole time." She didn't mention all the problems she dealt with daily; that was the nature of the business. "The place makes a profit, so technically that's your money. We can keep everything the way it is. You don't have to step foot on this property again if you don't want to."

"You're not hearing me. I've been thinking about it since my father passed last year, and I just don't see a scenario where I would want to keep this place."

She felt like she'd been punched in the gut. "But how could you do this? It's my home and my job. Plus we have seven employees who would be out of jobs, too, if you sold it."

Jesse shifted uncomfortably. "I'm sorry for that, but I can't keep something I don't want."

"Sure, you can. You've done a fine job of keeping it this past year and staying absent. We can keep everything status quo."

Jesse shook his head, "I hear you, but you should know I'm seriously considering selling it. I don't want you to get your hopes up that I'll change my mind."

"Wow. Message received." Rose felt all the old painful feelings rush back; the heartache and sadness she'd lived with after he'd left her. Eventually, she'd picked herself up and moved on with her life. But now he was back and threatening to sell the place, and a new kind of hurt moved in. Not just the fear that she'd lose her home and job, but that she'd lose the life she loved, as well.

Jesse's news settled like a dark cloud over them. They grew awkwardly silent. He cleared his throat. "I think I better head out." Jesse fished around in his pocket and pulled out his car keys.

It was probably a good idea. Rose worried she was on the verge of saying something she might regret. Instead, she said, "You know, the house is full of your dad's stuff. Your mom's, too, for that matter."

Jesse paused. "Yeah, I kind of thought that might be the case. Something else I've put off. Would you mind if I came back on Monday and start cleaning it out?"

Inwardly she had to laugh. How ironic that he was asking her permission when a minute ago he was threatening to sell the place.

"It's your place. You can do whatever you want," she said through gritted teeth.

"I know that, but I still want to be respectful of you."

"Sure you do." With her fists clenched by her sides, back ramrod straight, Rose stared him down.

Jesse wasn't stupid. He undoubtedly knew he'd said enough for one day. Thanking her politely, he stepped out of the halo of light they'd been standing in and made his way to the last car in the parking lot.

Rose watched his twin taillights drive away. Funny, it wasn't the shock of his reappearance or even the anger that he might sell her beloved farm that she felt at his departure. It was unease. As though her life was about to be changed forever, whether she liked it or not.

Monday morning, Jesse returned to the farm. As he drove up to his childhood home, the sunrise painted the scene in glorious light. The farmhouse and barn sat amid acres and acres of sunflowers that glowed a brilliant yellow in the morning sun. As a kid, he'd never noticed the beauty, but he'd been gone for so long. It was different to see it through the eyes of an adult.

Or maybe he'd never noticed its beauty because when he was fifteen, after his mom died, he'd walked around with his head down, hoping not to be noticed.

Jesse cleared his mind. He'd learned a long time ago to push back the bad memories. Usually that wasn't a problem, but being back at the farm brought them to the surface.

He focused instead on the sunflower fields. Many of the sunflowers were wilted and their leaves were turning brown. He'd noticed it on Saturday but hadn't given it much thought. He'd been so preoccupied with seeing crowds of people around his childhood home and distracted by seeing Rose after all this time.

Jesse scanned the rest of the farm. It wasn't just the flowers suffering. The grass was dry, too, like it hadn't seen rain in forever. It made sense. The last few months had been unusually dry for northern Florida. Summers generally consisted of daily afternoon showers that kept vegetation lush and green. This year, any rain showers had been few and far between. He'd never seen anything like it. As a result, the fire station had been getting more calls for brushfires. He hoped the drought would end soon.

The car came to a stop in front of the gift shop. His mind was heavy now that he realized how the farm was struggling. How had Rose been coping with this? Maybe it would be a relief to her if he sold the place.

Jesse climbed out of his car and looked around, expecting to see Rose or at least someone. The place was like a ghost town, the opposite of Saturday when visitors covered every nook and cranny of the farm. Jesse checked his watch and sighed. Seven o'clock in the morning was a little early, he supposed.

The gift shop was locked, so he went around the building. Rose said she lived above the shop—maybe he'd find her there? He took the steps two at a time and knocked on her door.

After a few minutes, the door flew open. "What are you doing here so early?" Rose snapped.

Jesse tried not to notice how adorable she looked

standing there in an oversize T-shirt, cotton shorts and her hair loose around her shoulders. "I couldn't sleep, so I thought I would come over."

She narrowed her eyes. "You couldn't sleep? Did it ever occur to you that maybe I could sleep?" She sounded put out. He couldn't blame her.

"Sorry. I figured you got started early, seeing how you live on the farm. Guess I was wrong."

Rose held her door partially open, shaking her head in annoyance. "Yes, normally we are up early, but Mondays are the one day I allow myself to sleep in just a bit. After the busy weekend, it's my recovery day."

"I'm sorry. Please go back to bed. I'll wait in my car until you get up, and then we can try again," he said, smiling.

"You think you're funny, don't you?"

He shrugged. "Sometimes. Though I prefer to call it charming."

"I've got news for you, that's not charm."

"Wow, somebody needs coffee."

She studied him. "You're not going away unless I let you in, are you?"

He flashed her another smile. Judging by the grumpy look on her face, she wasn't dazzled.

"Fine. I'm up now. Come on in." She opened the door wide.

Jesse stepped into her apartment. It was a small studio, with a bed, couch and kitchen crammed into one room. Not at all the dusty, unfinished space he remembered as a kid.

He shoved his hands into his pocket, unsure whether

he should sit. Instead, he followed Rose to the kitchen and leaned a hip against a counter.

Ignoring him, she grabbed a coffee tin from a shelf. On bare feet, she padded back and forth over the hardwood floors and grabbed a mug, cream and sugar. Jesse watched her, appreciating this side of her that he'd never seen when they were young and dating. All this time he had dreaded coming back, but now that he was here, she was a surprise. Even if she was a little angry about his absence…and a little mad that he wanted to sell the farm.

When the coffee was ready, Rose fixed herself a cup. She didn't offer any to Jesse.

"If you give me a minute to get dressed, I'll walk you over to the house and unlock it for you. I couldn't find a spare key, but I can get one made for you."

"Thanks, I appreciate it."

Rose grabbed some clothes out of a dresser and went into the bathroom to change.

Jessie decided to help himself to some coffee while he waited. Sipping the hot drink, he glanced at the pictures on her refrigerator and recognized her parents in one. Another photo showed Rose with his dad, Lolly and other staff, all wearing matching yellow Sunflower Farms T-shirts. His dad looked older than he remembered, but he also looked happy. Why did it sting to think he may have been happy?

Jesse took his mug over to the sofa and made himself comfortable. A few minutes later, Rose joined him wearing jeans and a clean T-shirt. She'd brushed her hair and pulled it up into a high ponytail. She was fresh-faced and too pretty. He forced himself to look away.

Rose pulled on a pair of worn-out boots, then set her empty mug in the sink and turned off the coffee-pot. Jesse gulped down the last few drops from his mug and set it down next to hers.

Rose watched him, her hands on her hips. "I see you helped yourself to my coffee."

"I didn't think you'd mind. There was plenty," he challenged.

Rose clucked to herself, then headed for the door with her back stiff and head held high.

It was going to be a long day.

Jesse knew better than to comment further. Following Rose down the stairs from her apartment, he tried to change the subject. "How's the sunflower crop this year? I couldn't help but notice everything looks dry."

Rose hit the bottom step and turned back at his question.

Jesse hadn't expected her to stop so abruptly and plowed right into her. Instantly, he reached out and steadied her. Hands lingering at her waist, he stared down into her blue eyes.

Rose stood with her hands at her sides like she was paralyzed. She didn't try to break away.

Why had he broken up with her when he left for college? He knew why, but for the millionth time he doubted his decisions when it came to Rose. It was something he had to live with, but standing next to her like this, he had his doubts.

A woman's voice broke through his thoughts, "Well, this is awkward."

Jesse and Rose both turned toward the interruption. A small elderly woman with short silver hair stood below the stairs, carrying a large paper bag in her arms.

"Grammy! What are you doing here so early?" Rose asked. She immediately stepped away from Jesse like she'd been caught doing something wrong.

"What am I doing here so early? What's he doing here so early?" the woman asked, nodding toward Jesse.

"Grammy," Rose admonished. "He just got here. Do you remember Jesse Cooper? We dated in high school. His dad owned this farm." She gave her grandma a peck on the cheek, then pulled the bag out of her arms.

Recognition lit her grandmother's face. "You were the football star Rose dated."

Jesse nodded. He hadn't thought of his football days in quite a while.

"You're the one who broke my Rose's heart."

Rose rolled her eyes. "Grammy, please…"

Jesse took the last step down and held out his hand. "Yes, ma'am. I suppose that's me. Nice to see you again, Mrs. McFarland."

"Oh please. You make me sound like I'm eighty years old." She shook his hand. "You can call me Grammy like Rose does."

"I didn't know you were stopping by today. What did you bring?" Rose asked as she peeked in the bag.

"I was cleaning off a bookshelf and thought I'd bring you some of my favorites."

Rose pulled out a cookbook and a hardback about

crocheting. Her brow wrinkled in confusion. "Thanks, Grammy, but I'm not sure I need these…"

"Go on and take them. I taught you to crochet when you were little. And cookbooks are always handy. There's a few more in there you'll like."

Rose put the books back in the bag and smiled at her grandmother. "Do you have time for coffee?"

"No, honey. I have to get going. I'm meeting Sally at the YMCA for water aerobics."

"That sounds fun. I'm glad you're trying new things," Rose said.

"We'll see. I just hope it's not full of old people."

Jesse glanced at Grammy to see if she was serious. Her face was completely straight.

"Okay," Rose said. "Next time, let me know you're coming, and maybe you can stay awhile."

As soon as Grammy left, Rose sighed and shook her head at the bag of books.

"What's wrong?" Jesse asked.

"She does this all the time. She cleans out a closet, and I end up with the junk she doesn't want to throw away."

"Maybe she just thinks you need to learn how to cook," Jesse joked.

Rose gave him a dirty look. "Not funny, Jesse Cooper. Come on, I have stuff to do."

"Now you have stuff to do? I thought it was your sleep-in day," he teased.

"I'm going to ignore that." She started toward the main house. For someone so much shorter than him, she sure could walk fast.

"What are your plans today?" Rose asked him over her shoulder.

"I thought I would go through the stuff in the house and start packing it up."

"There's extra boxes in the gift shop if you need them." Rose let him into the house, then left to do chores.

As Jesse walked from room to room, memories of his past swept through his mind. An electric hospital bed sat in the middle of his parents' room. A wheel-chair and a walker stood in another corner. It was all a stark reminder that his dad had been ill before passing away from cancer.

Had Rose been his only caretaker? Jesse realized he'd never asked.

He walked over to the closet and saw that it was full of clothes. His dad never cleared out his mom's stuff. He'd never let her go.

And he'd blamed Jesse for her death.

Jesse blamed himself, too. He'd been fifteen and learning to drive. He and his mother were coming home from church when another car had swerved and hit them. The collision had sent their car off the road, and it'd flipped several times, killing his mother. If he hadn't insisted on driving, she would have lived. It truly was all his fault.

Jesse backed out of the closet. Before he could stop himself, his legs carried him through the house and out the front door. He couldn't do it. The memories were too hard. His chest hurt.

In the distance, he heard the rumble of a motor. Rose was coming up the drive on a utility terrain vehicle, all windblown and beautiful. When she saw him standing on the porch, she pulled up and cut the engine. Her light blue eyes shone like diamonds in the morning sun.

"What are you doing out here? Already packing your bags and running away?" she asked.

"I'm not running away. I just need some air. It's harder than I expected being in that house."

"I was just about to go water the sunflower fields. Why don't you come help?"

"Are you looking for free labor?" he challenged.

She smiled at him. "Always."

"I can help water the fields. How hard can it be?" he said.

"That's right, you're a firefighter," she teased. "You should know your way around a water hose." She patted the seat next to her. "Come on, let's go. The fields aren't going to water themselves."

"Can I drive?" he asked.

Rose laughed. "Now you're just pushing your luck."

Rose watched Jesse walk around the UTV and hop on. The years had been kind to him. The lean teenager she'd known had filled out. What was already a good-looking face had matured into an incredibly handsome man.

She was angry with him, but if she were completely honest with herself, a tiny piece of her was actually thrilled to see him again.

Starting the engine again, she took off with a lurch. Jesse heaved forward.

"Hang on," Rose said automatically.

"Now you tell me," Jesse said over the noisy engine.

"Don't be a baby."

"You should have let me drive."

"You don't know where you're going," she said.

"I drove the hayride all day Saturday. I think I know the layout of the farm like the back of my hand."

"That's just one big circle. You don't know the short-cuts anymore."

Rose took a less-used path through the sunflower fields. The big blossoms and long stems whipped past them in a blur of yellow, green and brown. When they reached the outskirts of the farm, she rolled to a stop next to a large crop sprinkler, jumped out and dragged it down the row of flowers. Jesse followed her out of the UTV and waited as she positioned and started the sprinkler. When she finished, she gave him a pointed look. "What are you waiting for? Make yourself useful."

He shook his head. "Why are you doing this by hand?"

"You're here for ten seconds, and you already know better?"

"It's a simple question. I just don't recall ever having to water the sunflowers by hand when I was a kid. That's what the irrigation system was for."

"We've had some problems with the irrigation system this past year."

"Really, what kind of problems?"

She thought about evading the question, but there was no way to dance around the truth. "The irrigation system doesn't work."

"Have you had anybody out here to look at it?"

"Gee, I never would have thought of that. Now did you come out here to question me or to help?" Rose hated being questioned. She didn't know if it was the fact that she was a woman, young or short, but she always felt like men didn't give her enough credit. Like she couldn't manage a large successful farm or deal with the problems that came with it.

"All right, I told you I would help. I'll help."

Rose swallowed the retort on the tip of her tongue. They had work to do. "The sprinklers run every three rows. Go ahead and set up the next sprinkler, and we can alternate until we get to the end," she said.

"I can do that."

"Great, let's get to it."

Jesse gave her a funny look, then said, "You know, I don't remember you being this bossy when we dated."

Rose lifted her chin up a notch. "I'm sorry if I come across as bossy. You have to understand I'm not the same girl you dated all those years ago. I'm all grown up, and I have a farm to run. I'm used to giving orders. Everyone and everything around here depends on me and the decisions I make. I don't have time for people to question me at every turn."

With that, she pivoted briskly, her long ponytail flying over one shoulder as she stomped off.

For the next thirty minutes, they set up sprinklers and successfully avoided conversation until they headed back to the UTV. Jesse didn't ask to drive this time but sat silently next to her in the passenger seat.

Rose glanced at him as he pushed a hand through his damp hair. His clothes were drenched from moving the sprinklers, which was rather comical. She suppressed a smile. She'd moved those sprinklers enough that she had it down to a science, leaving her dry as a bone, but he looked like a drowned rat.

Jesse stared straight ahead.

Rose giggled, then started laughing so hard her eyes watered.

Slowly, Jesse turned his head, and with a stoic face asked, "What's so funny?"

Rose wiped her eyes when she could talk again. "I thought firefighters knew how to handle a water hose."

"I don't know what you're talking about," Jesse said stiffly. "I handled the sprinklers just fine."

Rose couldn't help but grin at the man. "Sure you did." She started the UTV, but this time he was ready and grabbed the side to brace himself.

Rose couldn't resist. "Hey, if you stick your head out the side, maybe the wind will dry you off."

"My luck, you'd drive past a tree and nail me in the head."

"I would never," she said, all innocence.

Rose took a dirt path to the edge of the property, where the land bordered a lake. She came to a stop near the water. The morning light reflected off the surface in a million sparkles.

Jesse's dark eyes passed over the area. "I'd forgotten about this place," he said quietly. "Man, it looks just the same as when we used to come out here."

Rose's earlier irritation was forgotten. Laughter had a way of making a person feel better. "Nothing much has changed. Though the water level is lower because of the drought the last few months," she said.

Jesse surveyed the water. "You're right, it is lower."

"We had some good times out here swimming, sunbathing and hanging out," she said.

"Yeah, good times. I thought I was all grown up because I could invite a few friends over to the lake, listen to music, and stay out late." He laughed.

Rose cut off the engine to the UTV. "You want to go walk out on the dock?"

"As long as we're here…"

They strolled down the dock side by side, Rose keenly aware of his closeness. The wood boards were faded from years of Florida sunshine and creaked under their weight.

"Do you ever come out here anymore?" Jesse asked.

"Not really. We're always busy, and I just don't have the time. I wish I did, though. Now that I'm here, I realize I've missed it."

They reached the end, and Rose sat down with her legs crisscrossed, feet tucked under her thighs. Jesse sat next to her, dangling his long legs over the dock edge. Casually he leaned back on his palms and faced the water. The sun had started to heat up the day, but occasionally a soft breeze stirred the air. For a few minutes they sat in silence.

"What are you thinking?" Rose asked.

"I guess mostly that it's a different way of life out here at the farm. I'd forgotten that part. I've become so accustomed to living in Jacksonville, within walking distance to restaurants and stores. I've gotten used to the noise. You know, cars, people, stuff like that. Out here, it's peace and quiet."

"Mostly peace and quiet, unless you're here on the weekend, and then it's busy. But you're right. It is a different way of life. Do you miss it?"

"I don't know. I didn't think so, but now that I'm here and see how beautiful everything is this time of year, it's eye-opening. But there's more to life than beauty. I had a tough time after my mom died. My dad made things real hard for me. That has a way of overshadowing everything else when I'm here."

"I can understand that. You went through a lot. Still, this place is a rare gem. Before we made Sunflower Farms more visitor-friendly, I traveled around the state to some other public farms for ideas. I came back here and slowly started making changes, with your dad's blessing. It was hard for him to let go of the reins at first, but he trusted me. We grew even more sunflowers and really started promoting them, then added our own touches like the classes and hayrides. It wasn't just picking strawberries anymore, but all the other stuff you see. Nobody else's farm is like ours. It's one of a kind. I want you to know that before you decide to sell it."

"I'm starting to see that."

"And you'll have to make sure to come back next weekend for the Sunflower Festival."

"You mentioned that the other day. What all goes into it?"

"We work with the church to put it together, and the proceeds go to families in need in the community. We've been doing it for about five years now. This year it's for a young family who was displaced from their home because of a fire. You may know them. Johnny Taylor's family? He graduated a couple of years ahead of us in high school."

Jesse sat up straighter. "Yeah, I do remember him. We played football together. You're not going to believe this, but that fire was in my district. It was in the middle of the night, and the place completely burned down. Fortunately, his family escaped along with all their pets."

Rose couldn't believe it. "What a small world. His mom goes to my church. She told us about the fire. Johnny and his family have been staying with her. They could use the money to help start over while they wait for the insurance to come through."

"I'd like to do something for them. Maybe I can help in some way with the festival."

"That'd be great. It never seems like we have enough volunteers, it's always so busy." Rose gasped at a sudden thought. "Oh…is there any chance you could bring out a fire engine for a day?"

"Yeah, I don't see why not. I'll check to make sure there isn't anything we're already committed to that weekend, but I'm sure we could do it at least one day. And I might be able to find a couple of volunteers to help man it."

Rose clapped her hands and beamed at him. "The kids will love it. Can they go inside the cab and crawl around the truck?"

Jesse grinned at her, clearly amused. "I think that could be arranged. And we can bring some of the gear and let them try it on."

"That'll be a huge hit. Thank you." For the first time since he'd arrived, Rose felt herself soften a little toward Jesse.

"Don't thank me yet. Let me make sure we're available first."

"I have confidence in you. I'll pencil you in," she teased.

"Well, in that case, I guess we have to be there," Jesse said with a chuckle.

They grew quiet again. Across the lake a white egret stood gracefully in the water close to shore. Every now and then he pecked at the water. Some crows cawed from the nearby treetops. The sun hid behind fluffy white clouds that kept the heat at bay. Jesse watched his surroundings in silence.

"I still can't believe you would consider giving this place up. This farm. It's my whole life. Please don't sell it," she said.

Jesse's eyes went from the lake to hers as he grew serious. "I understand that but I don't know if I can do what you're asking."

"If you sell it, you'll break my heart all over again. This time you'll take away my home and my job."

"You make it sound like it's such an easy decision. But it's not."

"Please consider all the people working here. There's seven employees, plus the seasonal help that depend on the extra money."

"I'll consider all of that in my decision," Jesse said. He shifted his attention back to the lake.

Probably better to let him think on that for a while.

Rose checked her watch. "It's getting late. We better head back. I have some things I need to do."

"What, more watering?"

"Actually, I do have to move the sprinklers in an hour, so if you dry out by then, maybe you can help."

Jesse laughed. He looked down at his clothes. He was already dry from the warm sunshine. "I'll help if you need it."

"I'm kidding. I'm sure you need to get back to clearing out the house."

They both got up and walked back to the UTV in silence. Jesse took his place in the passenger seat. On the way back to the house, they chatted about the different sides of the business and what crops did well on the farm and which didn't. Jesse had grown up around it and had a wealth of knowledge. He asked the right questions and understood the highs and lows of farming more than anyone. It really was a shame that he didn't seem to want to take over the farm after his father.

"Have you completely given up on fixing the irrigation system?" he asked her at one point.

Rose felt her shoulders drop. "Trust me, we've looked at it. We've repaired it many times, but it's old and it needs to be replaced. No more Band-Aids are going to work. And that's going to be expensive."

"Maybe it's a sign that it's time to sell."

"That's not a sign. It's just life. Things break, and you have to replace them."

"In this case, it should have already been replaced. Everything's so dry. The farm can't go without an irrigation system."

"It's autumn. Leaves turn colors, the grass dies. It's normal. You're making more out of it than it is." But she knew he was right. Normally northern Florida was still lush green in October.

She hated that Jesse had noticed the dry crops. The staff had been killing themselves watering the fields by hand for months, and honestly it could have been so much worse. She knew they could have lost it all.

It made her look bad, like she was incompetent at running the farm. Rose hated that the most.

"Selling this place wouldn't be the worst thing in the world," Jesse insisted. "You have an agriculture degree and a ton of experience. There's so much you could do. You could own your own farm."

She frowned at him. "I don't want another farm. This is my home."

They drove the rest of the way in silence. When Rose parked at the main house, Jesse said, "Thank you for taking me to the lake." His short black hair had dried and was now windblown in the front. It made him look younger. Rose had a flashback of the teenager she'd been in love with.

She shook off the memory. "You're welcome," she said coolly.

"Don't be mad, Rose. We should be able to talk about selling the farm like two adults."

"I don't know what you mean. I'm talking, and I'm listening…just like an adult."

Jesse climbed out of the vehicle and squinted down at her in the bright sunshine. "I can see that. I just want you to consider all sides. It could be a relief to let this place go. Especially in light of the irrigation system needing to be replaced." With that, he double tapped the roof of the UTV and backed away as if to signal her to go. At the last second, he added, "Oh, hey, would you mind if I come back tomorrow with some of my things? I have the week off and could probably get more done if I just stayed."

"It's your house. Do what you want," she said.

"I know. But I didn't want to step on your toes."

"I have pretty tough toes. I think I'll be okay." She dug in her pocket, pulled out the house key and threw it at him.

He was quick and caught it next to his head then gave her a stunned look.

"Keep the key so you don't have to wake me up to-morrow," she said.

Rose drove away before he could say anything else. It stung that she had to admit the irrigation system didn't work. She should have found a way to pay for a new one. She was also mad he'd been gone for so long and that he was thinking about selling the place. She hadn't worked all these years to turn this place around, only to have him thoughtlessly sell it. If that happened, she would be devastated.

Chapter Three

The alarm went off before the sun came up. Rose hit the clock to end the torture and rolled over with a groan. Unbidden, thoughts of Jesse sprang to mind. Sitting next to him at the lake yesterday brought back more memories than she'd been prepared for. Maybe it hadn't been such a good idea to take him there.

Rose got dressed, then left her apartment to be greeted by the sunrise lighting the sky. Glorious shades of pink and peach hung over the vast fields of colorful sunflowers. As dry as the conditions were, somehow they'd managed to keep the farm alive. Rose knew that had been an answer to prayer.

She also prayed for a solution to the irrigation system, and she prayed for rain. She was still waiting for those prayers to be answered.

Everything was quiet on the farm. The employees weren't due for another hour, and she had the place to herself. There was an autumn chill in the air this morning, but by afternoon, the day would be warm and sunny.

Rose started her morning with the usual chores. She fed the animals, led the horses out to pasture, milked Betsy, then let her join the horses. Once the barn was empty, she cleaned out the stalls, took fresh hay to the goats and spent a few minutes petting them. Lastly, she let the chickens out of their coop. The friendly hens walked in a line down the coop ramp, clucking loudly, as if greeting her.

"Good morning, ladies," Rose said to the hens, then added "and you too, Rocky," when the rooster pranced by. She was rather fond of the chickens, having raised each one by hand. When the coop was empty, she collected a basket of eggs.

Back at her apartment, Rose made scrambled eggs and toast, then set the rest of the eggs aside for Grammy.

After breakfast, Rose left her apartment and went downstairs to her office in the gift shop. The room was small, with her desk and cabinets taking up most the space. One window had a view of the parking lot, and on the other wall the window faced the sunflower fields. Rose sat down at her desk, grabbed a pencil and her Sunflower Festival binder, and went through her to-do list. She had everything planned, practically down to the minute, to get ready for the festival starting on Friday. There were only three days left for preparations. That made her a little nervous, but she knew they would pull through. The past four years, the festival has been a success. This year would be no different.

Absently, Rose chewed the pencil eraser as she reviewed her notes, then checked off some completed items. She sent reminder texts to the church members who had volunteered to do setup and to work at the festival. Then she called the pastor to confirm the plan to recognize the Taylor family in church on Sunday, and to announce the Sunflower Festival was raising money for them.

When Rose was finished, she put away the notebook and spent half an hour paying bills for the farm. She wondered if Jesse would be the least bit interested in looking over the books, seeing how much money was coming into the farm and how much was going out.

Rose said a silent prayer to God to continue to provide and to allow them to stay open.

Suddenly, her phone buzzed with a text. One of her employees, Justin, was calling in sick again. Rose sighed. She liked Justin. He was a good kid, but now there was more work for the rest of them and with the worst possible timing. With the festival coming up, everyone already had extra duties, and she really needed his help clearing a fallen tree from the garden. She shook her head in frustration.

Just then, a car drove up. Rose glanced out the window to see Jesse parking his car. Grabbing a bag from the car, he went around the gift shop and headed to the farmhouse.

He'd only brought a small duffel bag? What about food? Had he thought that far ahead? And was he really planning to sleep in his old dusty room?

Rose finished up with her office work and went back upstairs to her apartment to grab some clean linens for Jesse. Before heading out the door again, Rose stopped in front of a mirror to check her appearance. Out of habit, her hand smoothed over her hair, even though it was still neat. Why did she care what she looked like?

Just because Jesse Cooper was back, didn't mean she needed to look perfect.

Rose left the apartment, headed over to the main house, and stopped at the front door. When James Cooper lived there, she'd always knocked before entering. At some point in James's last year, she'd stopped knocking. He'd become so ill from cancer, she'd found herself over at his house all the time to help him. The formality of knocking had long been forgotten.

Never would she have imagined she'd be back on that same doorstep, knocking once again. This time with Jesse on the other side. Rose rapped on the door, waited a few minutes and when Jesse didn't answer, walked in.

Jesse set his bag down on the bed and turned to take in his surroundings. His bedroom was exactly as he'd left it as a teenager. How many hours had he spent here, staring up at the ceiling? Sadness and guilt would consume him as he'd replay the accident in his mind, over and over. Even though the police had told Jesse it hadn't been his fault, he'd always felt it was. Even worse, his dad had blamed him.

Jesse heard footsteps and turned toward the door. He half expected it to be his father. Dread washed over him like he was fifteen again. When Rose appeared in the doorway, Jesse sighed in relief.

"Hey there," she said. She seemed to be holding a stack of sheets in her arms.

Jesse quickly pushed aside his dark thoughts. "Good morning."

"I see you're here early again," Rose said. She was

dressed casually, with her hair up in the same tight ponytail that showed off her perfect oval face. Her big blue eyes studied him. Even in faded jeans and a T-shirt, she was a knockout.

"Yeah, but I came straight to the house this time. You can't blame me for waking you up." He smiled.

"No, I can't blame you. Instead, I can blame the million and one things I need to get done today," she said. "I've been up since before dawn."

"I got up early, too. I couldn't sleep again last night. After being here yesterday and with everything I need to do this week, there's so much spinning around in my head. I've also been thinking about the irrigation system. I want to look at it. Maybe see if there's anything I can do."

Rose's hackles seemed to go up. "Don't you believe me when I say it's beyond fixing?" she asked.

"Of course I believe you, but if there's any way I can help, I want to. I grew up around it, and more than once I was forced to help my dad work on it."

"Fine, but it's a waste of time. We've done everything."

Jesse shrugged. "Okay, then it's a waste of time. But at least let me try. I really don't mind."

Rose narrowed her eyes. "I hate it when you're nice. After the way I left things with you yesterday, you're making me look bad."

Jesse chuckled. "Come on, Rose, you could never look bad."

She grew silent and put a hand up to her hair as if to smooth it down. Was that a blush on her cheeks? Finally, she shoved the stack of linens at him. "Here. This is for you if you're sleeping here tonight. Clean sheets and a quilt."

"I hadn't even thought that far ahead, to be honest. I appreciate it."

"You're welcome. I saw you only had one bag with you. Not sure what you plan to eat, but hey, that's not my problem." She chuckled.

Jesse shrugged, then laughed. "I'll figure it out. Thank you for the clean sheets." He realized he wasn't sure what else to say. It had been easy to be around each other when they dated, but now it felt a little awkward.

"I'm heading out, now. Come find me if you need me," she said. Maybe she felt the awkwardness, too.

Jesse watched her leave, then glanced down at the stack of sheets she'd handed him. He lifted the sheets to his nose and the freshly laundered scent made him smile.

He made the bed, then opened his duffel bag and hung a couple of shirts on empty hangers he'd found in the closet. Then he moved on to his parents' room with a box full of heavy-duty garbage bags.

Jesse bagged his mom's clothes first. When he had about ten large bags, he decided to ask Rose if he could borrow her truck to take the clothes to the closest Goodwill, about twenty minutes away.

On his way out of the bedroom, he noticed a Bible on the nightstand. He didn't remember his dad ever reading the Bible. Jesse picked up the book and flipped through it, surprised by the handwritten notes in the margins of several pages. They were all in his dad's messy scrawl.

Rose had told him that his father had changed. Maybe he'd finally found some solace in faith. Jesse found that hard to believe. He set the Bible back down. It hurt to think about. Why couldn't he have changed when Jesse still lived with him?

He left the room, along with his troubling thoughts.

On his way to find Rose, he passed the two horses in the pasture. At the sight of Jesse, Missy trotted over to the fence. She nickered as if calling to him. Jesse stopped and petted her head and her soft, glossy neck. The horse seemed to enjoy the attention, nuzzling his hand.

Jesse had to admit, his spirits were lifting. Just being outside in the sunshine had a way of clearing his head.

"I'm sorry I don't have a treat, sweetheart. I'll try to scrounge up a carrot or apple later, I promise. What do you say about that?"

The other horse, Moe, was fifty feet away and ignored him. If he had an apple, no doubt Moe would be his best friend, too.

Jesse continued his search for Rose. Taking a chance, he headed toward the garden. It was easy to spot. The area was surrounded by a short, white picket fence, and an arbor stood at the entrance, covered in fragrant, blooming jasmine. Colorful flower beds lined the inside of the fence, and garden boxes grew a variety of vegetables and herbs in the middle of the garden. Toward the back, roses grew, resembling a proper English garden, meant to be strolled through and admired. Sprinklers watered the perimeter. Everything was lush and green, like the drought hadn't affected it at all.

The garden took up at least an acre. Jesse followed the stone pathway toward the roses. He passed through a tunnel covered in thick green vines and pink roses and emerged into a garden maze with rose petals littering the path.

How had he not known all of this was back here? In his time away, he'd missed so much. Who had created this? His father or Rose? He chose to believe the latter. For some reason, he didn't want to believe it was his father.

At last, Jesse found Rose in a back corner of the garden, where a large oak tree had fallen and crushed part of the picket fence. She was kneeling next to it, clearing out some of the small branches. Nearby, Grammy sat in the shade on a bench, chatting while Rose worked. Sunglasses sat on top of Grammy's head, holding her short hair back.

She gave Jesse a broad smile when she saw him. "You're still here?" Grammy asked in surprise.

"Yes, ma'am, I'm still here," Jesse said.

Rose paused in her work and looked up. A smudge of dirt stretched across one cheek.

Instinctually, he wanted to wipe it off. But he kept his hands to himself. Grammy might have a thing or two to say about that.

"I finally found you." Jesse said to Rose.

"I didn't know I was lost," she replied. She wiped the back of her gloved hand across her cheek and made the smudge worse.

Amused, Jesse smiled. She was adorable.

"This garden is amazing," he said. "I had no idea you had this many flowers back here."

Rose sat back on her heels. "Well, things change when you're gone for so long."

Rather than react to her tone, Jesse simply said, "This place is stunning."

She tilted her head, as if trying to decide whether he was being sincere. "Thanks. It's a lot of work." She sighed and gestured toward the fallen tree. "Sorry, I'm aggravated because Justin called in sick today, and he was supposed to help me clean up this mess. Plus, there's so much work to do before the festival this weekend. Grammy said she would help, but you can see her version of helping."

"I'm right here, darling. I can hear you," Grammy said from where she sat in the shade. "Besides, you know I'm only here for moral support."

Jesse scratched his chin as he surveyed the huge fallen tree. "I can help you for a bit. Do you have a chainsaw?"

"Really? You'd help me?" Rose asked, surprised.

"Yeah. Of course."

At once, Rose grabbed a chainsaw from the ground on the other side of the tree and handed it to Jesse. "Here you go."

It wasn't his first time using one. He studied it for a few seconds, then cranked it up and sliced through a thick branch like it was butter. He shut the chainsaw off and set the branch down to cut it up in smaller pieces.

"Impressive. They teach you that in firefighter school?" Rose teased,

"You forget I grew up here," Jesse said with a laugh. "I've cleared a few trees in my time."

For the next hour, he cut up the tree and Rose loaded the pieces into a wheelbarrow to haul to a stack of firewood nearby. They talked as they worked, while Grammy supervised from the bench.

"Did you create this garden by yourself?" Jesse asked, pausing the chainsaw to wipe sweat from his brow.

Rose threw another log into the wheelbarrow. "Most of it, yes."

"Where do you even start with something like this?"

"I've always loved gardening. Grammy and my parents gave me rosebushes for every special occasion. You know, because of my name and all."

"Very sweet," he said.

"Then when we decided to open up the farm and make it public, my brain got creative. I wanted to make an area people could walk through. Someplace nice to take pictures besides the sunflowers. I kept adding to it over time, until it grew into all this."

"It's magnificent. You've created something truly wonderful here. I can't imagine the amount of work it takes to keep this maintained."

"Yeah, it's a lot of work. The staff helps, but I end up out here every day. There's always something that needs to be weeded, picked or pruned. And with the drought, I've had to keep up with the watering."

"No wonder you need so much staff. This place has really grown."

Jesse threw the last of the wood into the wheelbarrow and hauled it away. When he returned to the garden, Rose was slowly pulling a large flowerpot across the ground.

"Need help with that?" he asked.

"That would be great," she said, panting.

Jesse helped move the pot. "There you go," he said as he brushed his hands off. "You know, I wanted to ask if I could borrow your truck to haul a load of clothes up to the donation center. Is that okay?"

"Sure, you're welcome to use it. I guess that means you're making progress in the house?"

"A little. I managed to clear out my mom's clothes, but that's about as far as I got." He didn't mention that he was dreading touching his father's things.

"I can't believe your dad left your mom's stuff there all these years," she said.

"I know. He never could deal with her death, but you already knew that." Jesse took a deep breath and let it out in a sigh.

Rose offered him a crooked smile. "I do. I'm sorry."

"Don't be. I knew this would be tough. It just stirs up all those old memories I've worked so hard to forget."

"I know he was tough on you, but doesn't it count for something that he changed eventually? He did become a better person."

Jesse frowned.

"He wasn't always a bad guy, like you remember. He turned his life around," Rose said.

"Too little, too late."

"Is it really too late?" she challenged.

"As far as I am concerned. The man I lived with was a bad guy. You were his employee. He treated his employees decently, but he saved the meanness for me."

"I know how he treated you wasn't fair for a teenage boy who just lost his mother. And you have every right to those feelings. But you've carried this hurt and anger around for too long. When you left, it affected him. He may not have told you he loved you, but I promise you he did. Eventually he found his way to church, and that led him to God, and it changed everything about him. His attitude, his work, his view on life in general. He became a better person. It truly was wonderful."

"Forgive me if I find that hard to believe. He never went to church when I was growing up. It always was just my mom and me going. He'd stay behind to work the farm." But Jesse recalled the Bible he found in his parents' room. He kept that information to himself. He wasn't ready to admit that his father could change, much less forgive him.

Not today.

Desperate to change the subject, Jesse asked, "So, how about that truck? Can I borrow it now?"

"I'll have to run and get the keys for you. But before you go, could I ask one more favor? Could you help me move some more flowerpots?"

"She can use your big strong muscles," Grammy chimed in with a sparkle in her eye and a wink for Jesse.

Jesse pretended to look around. "Who me? Big strong muscles? You must be joking."

"Don't let it go to your head," Rose said with a laugh. "Come on, now help me. The pots probably weigh eighty pounds each with soil in them. I'm sure you could lift them without a hitch."

Jesse moved four pots, one by one. They were in fact heavy, but he pretended they weren't. Was he trying to impress her? That question he decided not to explore.

As Jesse set the last pot down, his cell phone vibrated in his pocket. He wiped his hands and reached for his phone. It was his realtor. Jesse walked a few steps away for privacy.

"Hey, Jesse, it's Ray," the voice said on the phone.

"Hey, man. What's up?" Jesse peered over at Rose. She was fiddling with the pots, too far away to hear anything.

"I've made some calls like you asked, to see if anyone was interested in buying the farm you inherited. I found an investor who's very interested. He even made an offer of $1.4 million."

When Ray told him how much the investor was offering for the farm, Jesse was pleased. It was a bit more than he'd originally expected he'd get. "That's not bad," Jesse said.

"Do you want me to accept and draw up a contract?"

"I—I had no idea there would be interest so soon. I mean, I just got here. There's a ton to do before the house will be cleared out and ready for a new owner."

"I don't think that'll matter. This is a well-known commercial builder. He's not buying it to live there. If I had to guess, they're planning to bulldoze it and build a strip mall or a housing development."

Jesse's eyes went back to Rose, who was watering the flowers he'd just moved. Could he really sell the farm out from under her? She'd lose her home and everything she'd worked so hard to create.

It was a good offer, though. If he passed it up, another one might not come. The housing market was in a slump. This could be his only chance.

Ray went on, "They'll need an answer soon."

"I have to think about it. This is a huge decision, and it impacts other people, not just me. When do I need to decide?"

"As soon as possible, but if you need to think about it, I'm sure you can tell them next week at the latest."

"Okay. I'll give you a decision by then." Could he really sell the farm? What would that mean to Rose?

Jesse got off the phone and walked back over to Rose and her grandmother.

"Everything okay?" Rose asked as she turned off the hose. She knelt to pull up a couple of rogue weeds that dared to grow near a rosebush.

"Just some business. Nothing major." Jesse knew he would need to tell her about the offer, but it could wait. He needed to think about it first. Besides, every time he brought up selling the farm, it only made her angry. If he sold it, would she ever forgive him?

Rose stood up from her weeding and took off her gloves. She surveyed the garden and realized she wouldn't be able to get everything done. It was a good thing Jesse had agreed to help, otherwise it would have taken her the entire day to clean up the fallen tree. She'd still have to find time to fix the fence. There was never enough time in the day to do everything.

"I'm at a good stopping point," she said to Jesse. "Let's go get those truck keys for you." She turned to Grammy. "Are you ready to head back?"

"I guess I am. Never mind I was enjoying spending time with my granddaughter."

"We can still spend time together. You can come up to my apartment for some lemonade," Rose offered.

Grammy rose from the bench and straightened her shirt, then pulled her sunglasses down over her eyes. "No, I think I'll leave now and drive back to my house. I have things to do."

Rose shook her head. She'd just said she wanted to spend time together. Her grandmother was a contradiction sometimes. Maybe that was where Rose got it from. With Jesse back in town, her emotions were all over the place...angry, excited, happy to see him, unhappy to see him.

Rose and Jesse said goodbye to Grammy at her car, then dropped off the wheelbarrow and tools in the barn and headed to her apartment.

Rose tried to center herself. She was stronger and smarter than ever, and she could take care of the farm on her own. Never mind the endless problems that always seemed to be popping up. With a little bit of sweat, hard work and prayer, she'd get by. She always had. She didn't need a man to help her.

She didn't need Jesse Cooper.

The thing was, she had appreciated his help with the downed tree in her garden. But she needed to remember that his visit was only temporary. At the end of the week, he'd pack up and be gone once again.

When they reached her apartment, Rose ran upstairs to grab the keys, leaving Jesse outside in front of the gift shop. Glancing in a mirror on the wall, she came to an abrupt halt. There was a streak of dirt on her cheek. How long had that been there? Surely Jesse had seen it. He must think she was some country bumpkin who was dirty and sweaty half the time.

Running into the bathroom, she washed her face and hands. Her face rosy from a good scrubbing, she checked her hair quickly, satisfied to see her ponytail still in place. Grabbing the truck keys on the way out, she closed the door behind her and came to a stop.

At the bottom of the stairs, Jesse leaned against the wooden rail, his long legs crossed at the ankle and his elbows on the rail. He looked carefree and at peace as he watched her descend the stairs. You would never know he was struggling with his past. The man was a pro at hiding his feelings.

The Jesse she knew in high school had seemed like a normal teenage boy who loved sports and made decent grades. He'd been one of the most popular boys in school, fun and happy—until the accident happened. He'd lost his mother and childhood in one fell swoop.

Rose reached the bottom of the stairs and tossed him the keys. It was the same old truck that Jesse's dad had used on the farm for as long as she could remember.

"Here you go. It's parked out front. I trust you know how to drive a stick?"

Jesse gave her a look. "If I recall, I was the one that taught you how to drive that truck."

Rose laughed. "You're right. Now I'm the one wincing when some new hire grinds the gears." She tucked a loose strand of hair behind an ear. "I suppose the truck is yours now. I hadn't realized until now."

Jesse raised his brows as if it had not occurred to him, either. "I suppose you're right. But just so we're clear, I would never take the truck from you if you don't have another of your own."

"Don't worry, I have a car," she assured him.

"Okay then." He looked relieved.

"Hey, thanks again for helping with that tree. Could I bother you with one more thing? When you get back, could you help me pull some boxes out of the warehouse? I need to start decorating for the Sunflower Festival, or it'll never all get done by the weekend. I was going to ask one of the staff to help with some of the bigger boxes, but since you're here, would you?" She smiled sweetly, hoping that would help convince him.

"Yeah, of course. Do you want to do it now, before I go?"

"I would love to get started if that doesn't mess up your schedule."

He rubbed his chin. "It'll delay me from cleaning out my dad's things… So in that case, I'll definitely help you. Anything to avoid that haunted house."

Rose chuckled. "You're incorrigible."

He waggled his brows. "No, I just really don't want to clean out that room."

"Well, I know better than to pass up free help if you're

willing. Let's take the truck to the warehouse. You can drive."

"Sure, you let me drive the old beat-up truck but not the UTV yesterday," he kidded.

She laughed.

At the warehouse, Rose entered a code in the keypad, opened the door and flipped on the light. The boxes were stacked in the back, and Jesse's eyes took in the large pyramid before him. The top row brushed the warehouse's twenty-foot ceiling. "We're moving all those?"

Rose rolled her eyes. "Come on. It's not that bad."

"I pictured two or three boxes, like what we'd put Christmas decorations in. There have to be thirty or forty boxes here," he complained.

"Yep, we take our Sunflower Festival very seriously," she joked.

Ignoring her attempt at humor, he said, "Well, let's get to it. Do you have a lift to get to the top boxes?"

"We have a ladder."

"A ladder? That's it? Seems dangerous."

"You'll be fine. You're a firefighter, I bet you're used to climbing ladders."

"I am, but that's not the point."

"What is the point? I'm not asking you to climb the Empire State Building." Rose straightened her back, as if that would make up the difference in their height. Jesse was still taller, but she was used to being the boss, and he did not intimidate her.

"I know that. It's just this is how accidents happen. Whoever stacked this did not plan well. I would have done it completely different."

"Well, if you stick around, you can help me put it all away next week, and we can do it your way. But for now, let's get to it."

Jesse gave up and followed Rose to help her set up the ladder. Together, they pulled down all the boxes marked Sunflower Festival and loaded them on the truck. It took them two trips to haul everything from the warehouse to the barn, where the boxes would stay during setup for the festival.

Finally, Jesse left Rose to her unpacking while he ran his clothing donation errand. Even though she could have had some of the farm employees set up the lights, she chose to do it. She didn't mind the extra work because it was a good cause, plus she was picky when it came to decorating.

Rose started with the boxes of hanging lights and poles. They always hung thousands of lights for the festival's barn dance. Tediously, Rose tested each strand to make sure their bulbs worked, placing the faulty ones in a small pile to be worked on later. One of the Sunflower Farms employees, an older man named Tony, swung by to help. He put the poles together and began to set them up in the barnyard.

Before Rose knew it, Jesse was back. He walked into the barn with a takeout bag in one hand and a couple of drinks on a cardboard tray in the other. His eyes roamed the mess in surprise. "Wow. What's up with all the lights?"

"We're hanging them today for the festival."

"We?"

"Yes. *We*. Thanks for volunteering." She gave him a sly smile, daring him to protest.

"Funny, I don't recall volunteering."

"Don't worry. It won't take too long."

"Well, that changes everything," he said dryly. "Of course, I'll help if it won't take too long."

She eyed him. Had she gone too far? He'd already helped her out most of the morning.

Jesse continued, "Anyway, are you hungry? I picked up some lunch."

Rose put down the lights she'd been holding. "I'm starving." She stepped around a couple boxes and led Jesse outside to a picnic table. "What did you bring?" she asked as her stomach growled.

"I picked up some burgers from the new place next to the Goodwill. Thought we could try it out." They sat across from one another at the table, and Jesse handed her a soda. "Diet for you, if I recall."

"You recall correctly. Thanks." Rose took a big sip as she watched him open the bag and start pulling out their food. The smell of fresh fries hit her nose, and her mouth watered. "I can't remember the last time I ate fast food," she said as she popped a fry in her mouth.

"You're kidding, right?" He handed her a burger and a few napkins.

"No. I'm on the farm most of the time. Last time I checked, there are no fast-food joints here."

"You're probably better off. This stuff's not good for you," he said as he took a huge bite of his burger.

Rose shook her head. "Yeah, I can tell you're really worried about your cholesterol."

Jesse took another bite. His dark eyes watched her, dancing with humor.

Rose had to glance away.

She unwrapped her burger and took a smaller bite than Jesse. *Delicious.* They ate in silence, scarfing down their lunch, then lingering over the last of the fries.

"I was wondering," Jesse said at last, "how your parents are doing."

"They're good. Both fully retired now and enjoying it entirely too much. They bought an RV last year and have been traveling all over the country," Rose said. "I barely see them anymore, but it was their dream, so I'm happy for them."

A small smile touched Jesse's lips, "Good for them. They were always so nice to me, even before you and I started dating. When I would see them at church, they'd always ask how I was doing. They were good friends with my mom before…you know."

"They always were so fond of you and your mom," Rose agreed, not sure what else to say.

"Did they keep their house when they bought the RV?"

"They sold their house and bought a smaller place. They didn't need a big house and yard anymore for just the two of them. Their new place isn't far from here, which makes me happy because I like having them nearby. Even if they are gone half the time," she said.

"Are they traveling right now?" Jesse asked as he grabbed another fry.

"Yeah, they're finishing up a road trip out west. Mom keeps texting me photos. I'm so jealous. I don't know why they never took any of these trips when I was growing up." Rose took out her phone and showed Jesse a few of the recent ones of the Grand Canyon.

"Wow, looks amazing. It's so dry and different from Florida and our tropical climate here. It's like a whole other world."

"I know but if we don't get some rain soon, it'll be like the Grand Canyon here, too," Rose griped as she swiped through a few more pictures. "They should be home soon. They promised to be here in time for the festival this weekend."

"I'm sure you'll be glad to have them back."

"It does make me happy. I can't wait to see them."

"You were always lucky to have such great parents and the perfect childhood. You have no idea."

To Jesse's credit, he didn't sound bitter. His childhood had been good until the accident. Still…it was time to change the subject.

"So, seriously, you want to help me hang the lights?" she asked as she put her phone away.

"Sure thing."

She balled up her burger wrapper, tucked it into the white bag and then stood from the picnic table. Jesse shoved the last two fries in his mouth, threw his trash in the bag, too, and tossed it into a garbage can by the barn door. Then he followed Rose around the barnyard with a small stepladder, looping the lights in graceful swags between each pole.

Every now and then, Rose stepped back, eyed the swags critically, and if they didn't match perfectly, she made him adjust them.

"Nothing has changed," he said. "You're still the same perfectionist you were in high school."

"Who, me?" she asked. But deep down she knew he was right.

"Remember when we decorated for prom? It took twice as long as it should have because everything had to be perfect."

"You're exaggerating. It took twice as long because everyone was goofing off. Including you, mister."

He didn't bother to deny it, but simply moved the ladder to the next pole.

"That's perfect," Rose said when he had adjusted another long string of lights.

"I remember how pretty you looked," Jesse said casually.

Rose didn't know where that came from. Was he talking to her? She looked around and only saw Tony on the other side of the yard working on the poles. She was sure he wasn't calling Tony pretty.

Rose felt her face turn pink. "What?"

He glanced down at her. "Prom night. I remember how pretty you were. I felt like the luckiest guy to be with you."

Rose didn't know what to say. She just stared up at him, thinking about that night ten years ago. He remembered? And he thought she was pretty?

Jesse continued, "You wore a teal-colored gown and your hair was all fancy."

That broke the moment, and she laughed. "You thought my hair was fancy? That's what you remember?"

"Yeah. You fixed it different. It was up in some kind of updo, with soft curls all around your face."

"You're right. My mom took me to the hair salon to get it fixed all fancy, as you would say. And that dress, oh my, I loved that dress. I saved up all year, so I could buy it."

Jesse moved the ladder to keep stringing lights. "Do you remember that night? It was so much fun. And man, I liked you so much back then…" His words trailed off, as if he suddenly realized what he'd said.

Rose stood there speechless. That was what she remembered, too, including how much she'd liked him. But she didn't dare say it out loud.

Jesse looked down at her. Their eyes met and held. "I'm sorry about leaving you the way I did."

They weren't talking about the prom anymore.

"Are you?" she whispered, even though Tony wasn't within earshot of their private conversation.

Jesse stepped down from the ladder to face her, a string of lights held between them. It wasn't lost on Rose that she'd been telling him to forgive his dad, but she wasn't sure she could forgive Jesse.

"Just stop. Don't say anymore," she said.

"Stop? You want me to stop apologizing? For ten years, it's eaten away at me, the way I left you. Believe it or not, I loved you back then. But I had to go, and you couldn't come with me. I didn't want you to give up your dreams. I am sincerely sorry for what I did to you."

She saw the emotions on his face, the sincerity in his eyes. Rose took a deep breath. "Why are you saying this now?"

"Because now that I'm back home, I realize how badly I hurt you. I handled everything all wrong. I was young and dumb and selfish, and if it makes you feel any better, I missed you so much after I left."

"But not enough to come back," she said simply.

She saw the pain in his eyes, but she refused to feel sorry for him.

"It was complicated," was all he said. He stood still, looking at her a moment more, then went back to the ladder. Rose followed with the lights.

She didn't know how to respond. It had been complicated for her, too, but she hadn't left him. She wouldn't have done that to him.

It took an hour for them to put up all the lights. Jesse watched as Rose made sure every detail was perfect. Tony had placed a few of the poles in the wrong place, so she had Jesse pull them up and move them to make an exact square in the barnyard.

Jesse glanced over Rose's head at Tony, who rolled his eyes good-naturedly. Apparently, the man knew what to expect when working with Rose.

As they mounted lights around the barn doors and along the barn walls, Jesse listened to Rose and Tony joke around like old friends. Jesse guessed Tony to be about his dad's age. He actually liked him quite a lot after just knowing him a short time.

Finally, when Rose was satisfied, Tony went on his way to take care of chores and Jesse followed Rose back into the barn.

"Can you throw those in a box and carry them up to

my apartment?" she asked, pointing at about ten strands of faulty lights on the floor. "I'll see if I can get them working later. Here are some extra bulbs, put those in the box, too."

"Sure thing." Jesse packed up the lights, walked them over to her apartment, and set them down at her door. He glanced at his watch and saw that it was already after four. It was too early to call it a day, but he had no desire to go back to cleaning out the house again.

When he got back to the barn, Rose had unpacked several more boxes. It looked like a party store had exploded in the barn. Red, gold and orange decorations were strewn everywhere. How had that happened in the five minutes he'd been gone?

Rose was examining a large wreath made of straw and colorful autumn leaves when she spotted him. "There's so much more to do," she said.

"I can see that. You want some more help?" Jesse offered, though he had a feeling she'd already designated some jobs for him.

"I would love more help. I'll even throw in dinner later. That is, if you still like spaghetti."

Jesse grinned. "You remembered that's my favorite."

She grinned back. "Of course."

"I think I can be bought with food." He would have done it for nothing, but he kept that thought to himself.

"I thought so. You've more than earned it today." She handed him the wreath, then pulled an exact replica of it out of the box. "These go on the front of the barn doors. You'll see hooks already there to hang them."

Jesse took both wreaths and hung them on the barn

doors. He stood back to make sure they would be straight enough for Rose, tipped one a little more to the right, then nodded in approval. By the time he returned to Rose, she'd laid out six more identical wreaths.

"They're multiplying," Jesse said. "What are we doing with those?"

"Those go on the walls outside the barn, you'll see more hooks. You hang, I'll keep unpacking stuff."

Rose pulled out colorful autumn garlands to wrap around the poles holding up the twinkle lights.

"I see you have this down to a science," Jesse noted as he tied off the top portion. She wrapped the garland gracefully around the pole and secured it at the bottom. It was exactly the right length.

"Yep, we're careful taking them down and packing them each year, so we can reuse them. I have a system."

"Do you usually do all this by yourself?"

"No. Tony helps, but as you saw, he was more than happy to let you take over as decorating assistant this year."

Jesse laughed. "I can't blame him."

Rose pouted playfully. "Come on. This isn't so bad."

"No, it's not. He's the one missing out on the spaghetti."

"I don't usually make him spaghetti, so you should feel special," she teased.

"I do feel special."

"Besides, I saw the overnight bag but no groceries. I figured you didn't think as far ahead as dinner."

"It's embarrassing how easy it is for you to read me." They walked to the next pole and added garland. "What did my dad think of all this hoopla?" Jesse asked, glancing down at Rose.

She carried the box of garland to the next pole. "Hoopla pretty much describes what he thought. He didn't understand why we should go through all the trouble. He didn't mind us having the festival for a good cause, but he didn't see the need for the decorations, the dance, all the extra stuff. In his mind, it was extra work."

"I hate to say it, but I kind of agree with him."

"All the extra work, that's what makes it special. It can't be just another busy Saturday, with the same old classes and hayrides. We get this place all dolled up, like a church on Easter Sunday. We want people to remember it and come back next year. Our festival has gotten us noticed nationally. Every year, it gets bigger and we get more coverage. It's something special."

Rose's passion impressed Jesse. She was the backbone of Sunflower Farms and probably the reason for its success in recent years. He could see why his dad had put all his trust in her.

"I'm starting to think this place is lucky to have you," he said.

"No, I'm lucky to be here," she countered.

Later that afternoon, Rose released Jesse from his decorating duties. He watched her head off to take care of the animals, and when he was sure she was gone, he went back over to the tool cabinet in the corner of the barn.

He'd spied a new white picket fence panel leaning against the wall, waiting to replace the garden fence crushed by the old oak tree. Jesse grabbed the fencing and some tools and carried everything to the garden.

He wanted to do something nice for Rose. That morning, she'd been stressed over her employee calling in sick and having to clear that tree by herself. If he fixed the fence, it would be one less thing for her to worry about. He still wanted to check the irrigation system, but that would have to wait. The day was almost over.

Why was he doing all this? He hadn't planned on helping around the farm. He acknowledged there was something about rolling up your sleeves and getting your hands dirty, that spoke to him. He'd forgotten what it was like to be around nature, have the sun on your back, and to break a sweat through manual labor. What would it be like to be around this all the time as an adult? Jesse couldn't imagine. It was something he couldn't wait to get away from at eighteen but being here now, it made him wonder. He could see why Rose loved it but this was her world now, not his. He would never move back. As he worked on the fence, his mind went back to the conversation with his realtor. He wanted Jesse to make a quick decision about selling the farm.

Should he tell Rose about the offer he received? He didn't want to upset her more but he knew the right thing to do would be to tell her.

Chapter Four

Rose added the spaghetti to the boiling water on the stove, then stirred the tomato sauce bubbling in another saucepan. Anxiously she checked the time again. Why was she so nervous? This wasn't a date. It was just two old friends sharing a meal.

Two old friends with a history...

A few minutes later, she heard his knock. Quickly checking herself in the mirror, she tossed her loose hair over her shoulder and smiled. She walked over to the door to let him in. Butterflies fluttered in her stomach when he smiled at her from across the threshold.

"Hey there, come on in," she said as she opened the door all the way.

"Thanks. It smells delicious."

He walked past and Rose couldn't help but notice the scent of fresh soap. His hair was combed back and still damp. Like he'd just showered.

Rose inwardly shook herself. This was not a date.

"Don't get too excited," she said. "The sauce isn't homemade or anything."

"That works for me." He shoved his hands into his jean pockets. "I'm just glad you invited me, otherwise,

I'd be hightailing it to town right about now to pick up some fast food."

Rose laughed. "Have a seat. I just put the spaghetti in, so it'll be about ten minutes." She went back to the kitchen and checked the sauce one more time.

Jesse sat on the couch, stretched his long legs out and made himself comfortable. The studio was small enough for them to carry on a conversation with him in the living room and her in the kitchen.

"Thanks again for your help today," she said. "I'm not sure how busy you'll be the rest of the week, but there's plenty more to do if you have the time."

"I'll keep that in mind. I promised myself I wouldn't procrastinate tomorrow, so I plan on attacking my dad's bedroom. Maybe later this week I can help again."

"Honestly, I think it would be good for you to see what all goes into the festival, since this is your farm now. Maybe you'll want to come back here one day on a more permanent basis."

Jesse's face changed suddenly, like he wanted to say something but was holding back. Instead, all he said was, "Maybe."

They chitchatted some more while she drained the pasta, and they made their plates. Sitting at the kitchen island, Jesse ate heartily, helping himself to seconds before Rose had even eaten half her plate.

After a while, her nerves settled, and she felt that old comfortable feeling sitting next to Jesse. He had an easygoing personality and had always been fun to be around.

Quite the opposite of herself. The older she got, the

more uptight she'd become. Being in charge was a big responsibility. She had a lot on her shoulders with the farm, and making sure it was profitable was no small feat. It had been tougher when Jesse's dad was diagnosed with cancer. She'd watched him deteriorate for months until he couldn't care for himself anymore. That was when she stepped up, doing as much as she could to help him around the house. She began taking him to doctor appointments, pharmacy runs, and shopping for him. When it became too much for Rose to care for him and manage the farm, her dear friends, Mr. and Mrs. Dawkins from church, started making daily trips to the farm to help. The Dawkins would give Rose a break and would sit with James, while she worked on the farm. In his last two weeks of life, a local hospice caregiver came to the farm and helped as well. Finally too weak to get out of bed, James Cooper faded away. It had broken her heart to go through it with him, and it still hurt to remember it. Jesse had no idea how bad it had been.

A low whistle caught her attention. "Earth to Rose," Jesse said, waving his hand in front of her face.

Rose pulled herself out of the dark memory and glanced over at him.

"You okay?" he asked.

"Yeah. Just thinking."

"About what?"

"I'm not sure you want to know."

"Sure I do."

"I was thinking about your father and how sick he was at the end. How hard it was to take care of him and this place. By myself."

Jesse studied her. "You're right, I don't want to know."

"Do you think you'll *ever* want to know?" she asked patiently.

"I hope so. I'm just not there yet. Coming back to the farm was a big step. I'm still adjusting to the shock of being here again. I'll let you know when I'm ready to talk about him, and then I'll hear what you have to say," he said softly.

Rose nodded and went back to her spaghetti. It would do no good to push him. He might never be ready to talk about it. She, more than anyone, knew what Jesse had gone through with the man. But he never got a chance to see what a good man of faith his father had become. She wanted Jesse to know that. She wanted his dad to be remembered as a good person. Was that even possible? And why was it so important to her?

Because she knew he needed to forgive his father in order to heal his own wounded heart.

They finished eating in silence. At last, Rose picked up her dishes to carry to the sink, then gestured at Jesse's empty plate. "Are you ready for me to take that or are you planning on thirds?"

"I can have thirds?" he teased.

"With the way you eat, I'm sure you could make room for fourths."

He laughed lightly. "You think you know me so well. No, I'll pass on having more. I'm stuffed." He patted his stomach, then stood. "You made dinner, let me do the dishes."

Rose was surprised. "Who? You?"

"Sure. You forget I'm a bachelor. I've had to learn how to do my own dishes."

"Have at it then. I'll put the leftovers away, you wash."

Together, they made quick work of the cleanup. Rose packed the extra spaghetti and sauce into some plastic containers while Jesse washed the plates and pots. As he was finishing up, she pulled a towel out of a drawer and stood next to him to dry the dishes.

"I see the hens have been working overtime," Jesse said with a nod toward a basket of eggs on the counter.

Rose laughed. "Eggs are plentiful around here. I set those aside for Grammy today, and she forgot to grab them before she left. I'll take them to her tomorrow. She lives just down the road, like ten minutes away."

"One of the perks of living on a farm. Lots of eggs," Jesse said.

"One of the many perks," Rose added. "Help yourself to some if you want."

"Thanks. Maybe later." Jesse rinsed the last pot and set it on the counter for Rose to dry. "We make a pretty good team."

"Yeah, well, that was never the problem with us, if I recall," she said matter-of-factly.

"I suppose you're right. What we had was special." Jesse pulled the stopper and let the soapy water go down the drain. Drying his hands, he leaned his hip against the counter.

"Do you think you'll ever get married?" she asked. Personally, she didn't think she'd ever find anyone like Jesse again. That was the reason she'd barely dated since he'd left. No one ever could measure up to him.

"I don't know. I've dated, but it's never been quite right with anyone. Maybe one day, though. How about you? I'm sure there will be somebody out there for you. Someone better than me, that's for sure. I was nothing but a disappointment, I realize that now."

Rose put the last pot away in the bottom cabinet, then stood up and rubbed her forehead with a free hand. "Seems we're getting serious again. I guess it's inevitable when you have unfinished business like we do." She searched for a way to express what she felt. "Disappointment isn't the word I would use. You were everything to me. I loved you. When you left, I wasn't disappointed. I was shocked and heartbroken. That's what I was. Not disappointed."

"I'm sorry. I really am."

Rose stared at him. She could see his regret for his actions written all over his face—the way his jaw was set, how sad his eyes were, and the tight line of his lips. In a way, she hoped he felt bad. At the time, she'd felt worse.

Changing the subject, she asked, "Did you save room for dessert? I have some rocky road ice cream." Without waiting for an answer, she pushed away from the sink and grabbed the ice cream from the freezer. The brief rush of cold air felt good on her hot face.

When she turned back, she bumped into Jesse's chest.

Confused, Rose tilted her head up and searched his eyes. He took the ice cream from her hands and set it on the counter. Then he put his arms around her in a hug. Leaning down, he rested his cheek on the top of her head and just held her.

Rose was too surprised to say or do anything. Then slowly her arms circled his waist. Jesse sighed softly.

A long-forgotten sensation came flooding back... that feeling of contentment in his arms. She felt seventeen again, young and innocent. All the hurt she'd been carrying temporarily slipped away, as she gave in to her memories of the young man she'd once loved.

Jesse knew the minute Rose let her guard down. She went from stiff and unsure in his arms to soft and sweet. She was petite and even felt delicate in his arms, but he knew she wasn't weak. Quite the opposite. She had a backbone of steel. He wanted to protect her and keep her safe. He also wanted her to know how sorry he was for everything.

Leaving her had been the worst thing he'd ever done. And the stupidest.

Holding her in his arms brought back so many memories. He didn't move or say anything for a long time, too afraid he'd break the spell, and she'd push him away. He knew this would be short-lived. There was no doubt about that.

This could get awkward. He let her go.

She stepped back out of his arms, her eyes cast down.

He realized he wasn't ready to let go. He remembered the connection they'd once shared.

Before he changed his mind, Jesse reached out, lifted her chin and kissed her.

Hesitantly, Rose kissed him in return.

When he pulled back, she studied him. He wondered what she was thinking.

"I really am sorry for everything," he said.

"I know," she said simply.

Jesse was kind of hoping for more, like maybe she forgave him. Did he really expect one hug and a short kiss to change everything between them?

Rose picked up the ice cream again, grabbed some bowls and spoons and started scooping. Her movements were shaky as if he'd flustered her. Soon they were both sitting at the island with their bowls of ice cream.

When Jesse finished his, he stood up. "I better get going. I'm sure you've had enough of me for one day," he kidded.

She shook her head. "No. I hate to say it, but it's been nice having you around. When do you go back to work?"

"I'm off the rest of the week," he reminded her. "I'll go back Monday."

He thought he saw something flicker across her face. A touch of sadness, maybe.

"By the way, I confirmed the fire truck for the Sunflower Festival," he said. "They can come each day, and I've got a volunteer to help with the truck."

With the change of subject, she shifted back into business mode. "That's great," she said. "Do you think they could give some safety talks, too?"

Jesse gave her a peculiar look. "I thought people were coming here to have fun," Jesse said. "Being lectured on checking the batteries in your smoke alarms doesn't sound all that fun to me."

"When you put it that way, I guess not. I was just trying to think of how to make the most of it."

"Don't worry, we do this all the time. The guys will

bring the gear and let the kids try it on. My buddy Mike might be willing to tell some stories if he finds the right time for it. Either way, the truck is always a big hit."

"All right. I'll take your word for it. Thank you."

"Well, I better get going. Thanks again for dinner." He took his bowl to the sink and rinsed it out.

As Rose walked him to the door, he realized that he hadn't mentioned the offer on the farm. Things had been going so well… He hated to spoil the evening by bringing it up. But she needed to know.

"Rose, there's something else I wanted to tell you."

"It's been quite the night, I don't know if I can handle anything else," she said dryly.

"No, I'm being serious," he said, tension suddenly filling him.

"From the look on your face, I'm guessing it's not good."

"It can be good. It just depends on how you look at it." Uncomfortable, he shoved his hands in his pockets. "I've received an offer to buy the farm. You should know that I'm seriously considering it."

Rose looked crushed. "You would really sell this place?"

"Why would I keep it?"

"Because I'll run it. You won't have to lift a finger. It doesn't get much better than that."

"I don't want the farm."

"How can you say that? This is your legacy. It's been in your family for three generations. And your mother loved this place. You had fifteen good years here growing up when your mom was still alive. Doesn't that mean anything to you? All you ever focus on are the three years after her death!"

"Before she died we were actually a happy family. I could tell how in love my parents were. But then I ruined everything when I killed her," he said crudely.

Rose grabbed his arm. "You *didn't* kill her," she said firmly. "You were in a car accident. You were only fifteen and just learning to drive. Even an experienced driver couldn't have prevented that other car from slamming into you. It was an accident. Give yourself a break. It wasn't your fault."

"He blamed me."

"Your dad was wrong. He couldn't see past his own loss to act like the father he should have been. He shouldn't have blamed you. And you shouldn't blame yourself."

"All that doesn't matter now. He's gone, and I don't live here anymore. I live in Jacksonville, I'm a firefighter, not a farmer. And I think you should know, I've been offered a decent amount to sell the farm."

"You'll regret giving up your family legacy," she reiterated.

"No, I won't," he said, more out of stubbornness than anything. He didn't know if he would regret it or not. He still planned to think about it thoroughly before he decided what to do. The problem was, he had to decide by next week.

"Do you mind me asking, how much did they offer?"

"$1.4 million."

Rose didn't flinch. "I'll admit, that's a lot of money. But if you sell this place, you'll put seven people plus me out of work, and I'll lose my home and everything I love. For what? Money. I knew you could be foolish, but I never thought you were greedy, too."

"I'm sorry, Rose, but I'm not doing it to hurt you."

"Well, you would hurt me. Again."

"I can only say I'm sorry so many times. I've made no decision yet, so don't be mad at me. I'll let you know either way, when I decide."

"I'll be praying that you make the right decision this time," Rose said.

"Don't you get tired of all the problems that go along with running this farm? Fallen trees, droughts, broken irrigation systems, employees calling in sick. And those are only the problems I've seen in the few days I've been back. I can only imagine what else there is that you haven't told me about. If I sell this place, you wouldn't have to worry about any of it anymore. And just so you know, I would give you some of the money, so you could start over."

"You mean you'd give me a severance package," she said bitterly.

"Well… I—I…" Jesse tripped on his words. "That's not what I meant." But now that she said it, he supposed she was right. "I don't want you to worry about being kicked out on the street. You would have enough money to live on until you figured out what to do."

Rose's face turned red with anger. "You know, one minute you act like this great guy, helping me out today, even being charming. You apologized… We shared a kiss. Then you tell me you're still considering selling the farm, and it reminds me that I don't know you anymore."

"Come on, Rose. I'm the same guy you've always known."

"Yes, you are. You're the same guy that left me."

Rose opened her front door.

That was her cue for him to leave. Who could blame her for being upset with him?

"Thank you for dinner. I really appreciate it. I feel bad for leaving on a sour note like this," he said.

Rose closed the door on him.

Chapter Five

Carrying two mugs of hot coffee, Rose crossed the dry front yard and walked up the porch to the main house. She'd been up since dawn, feeding the animals and doing her morning chores. Out at the rose garden, she'd been surprised by the repaired fence where the fallen tree had been. She had a strong suspicion Jesse was the one who'd fixed it. The coffee was a thank-you for fixing it.

With time to cool off, Rose could see why he'd consider selling the farm. But it didn't mean she liked it. He thought this place was a lot of work, and it was, but it was worth it. Yes, things broke, and issues came up, but she dealt with them. And sometimes she worried about making payroll or paying the bills. Currently, they couldn't afford a new irrigation system, and because of the drought, it was the worst timing. But she couldn't let Jesse see her worries or he'd be even more convinced she couldn't manage the farm.

She needed to help him fall in love with the place so he would want to keep it.

Rose knocked on the front door.

After a minute, Jesse appeared at the door. Surprise lit his handsome face. "Hey. I wasn't expecting you."

"I come bearing coffee." She shoved a mug toward him.

"Thanks. You read my mind. I've been dying for coffee all morning. I can say with certainty, I did not plan well when I came out here from Jacksonville."

"Told you so."

"Yes, you did." Jesse took a big sip.

"You could have come to my place for some coffee," she said.

"Yeah, right. After the way we ended things last night? I figured if I asked you for a cup of coffee this morning, you'd throw it at my head."

She tried not to smile. A corner of her mouth lifted anyway. "Aren't you being a little dramatic?"

He lifted his brows. "You think?"

Rose laughed. "Okay, maybe not. Sorry about that. You just took me by surprise with the offer on the farm."

"I can understand that." He took another sip.

"But we're adults now, so I decided to put on my big girl pants and play nice. Maybe I can even talk you out of selling the place."

"You're welcome to try, but I'll have to do what I feel is best."

"I understand. And thank you, by the way."

"For what?"

"Fixing the garden fence. I know it was you." She shook her head. "I don't know where you found the time."

"No worries. It's not a big deal."

Rose looked past Jesse into the house. "It looks the same in there. I thought you planned to clear this place out?"

Jesse glanced over his shoulder. "It's a slow process. Don't forget I spent half the day yesterday helping you. Do you want to come in for a few minutes?" He held open the door for her.

Rose hadn't planned on staying, but she found herself nodding, nonetheless. She ignored the way it felt to brush his arm with hers as she passed him.

"I've been thinking about keeping the table," he said, following her into the kitchen. "I have a little one in my apartment, but this piece is much nicer."

"Then keep it. Though I will say, it is perfect for this space." Standing with one hand on her hip and the other holding her coffee, she surveyed the large kitchen. The solid farmhouse table had probably been in Jesse's family for a couple generations, made back when furniture was built to last.

"It does look like it was made for this room, doesn't it?" he said.

"Couldn't you just see yourself living here? Sitting at the same table you sat at as a kid...raising your own family?" she asked.

Rose could see the sadness wash over Jesse's face. "I've never thought about it. I mean, I want a family one day, but I never envisioned myself living here. I guess I always felt like my dad would live forever, which meant I would never come back here."

"I think we may have our lives planned out. But

often God has something else for us. Nothing we can imagine, and often much better."

"That sounds like something my mom would have said. She always had words of wisdom for me like that."

"She was a smart woman."

"Wonderful, too." He ran a hand through his short hair and walked up to the window. He stared absently at all the lights and decorations they'd put up around the barn, but she wondered if he was actually seeing them. "Something about being back makes me think of her," he said at last. "You know, I dreaded coming here for fear I would be overwhelmed with the memories of him, but I never considered I'd be blessed with memories of her, too."

He glanced back at Rose. This big strong man in front of her suddenly looked vulnerable, and her heart went out to him.

"I think you're going to be okay," she said. "What you're going through, it's what a lot of people go through when they lose their parents. It's part of the grieving process."

"But I'm not grieving him."

"Aren't you? I think in your own way, you're coming to terms with losing him again."

Jesse just shoved a hand in his pocket and turned back toward the window.

It was clear he was finished talking. Rose strolled around the kitchen, quietly opening cabinets and the pantry door to see what else he might need for the week. She stopped short at the coffee maker on the counter.

"Ah, look here. I thought you couldn't make coffee. You had a coffee maker hiding in plain sight," she said.

He smiled over his shoulder, "Yeah, I found that, too, but there's no coffee. I need to make a grocery run today, so I don't have to keep bothering you."

She shook her head. "You're not bothering me. I told you last night, it's been nice having you around." She was glad to see him sort of back to his happy-go-lucky self. "Show me what you've done so far in the house."

"Sure, come on back." Jesse led her to the main bedroom.

Rose felt a lump in her throat, and her eyes watered as she looked around. Unlike Jesse, she missed James Cooper. After he'd found God, a kind of peace and healing had settled over him. The difference in him had been like night and day. Everyone around the farm noticed.

"I have some time this morning. Would you like help?" she asked.

"If you're offering, I'll take it. I feel like I'm up to my eyeballs in clothes."

"I wonder if the Taylor family could use any furniture, since they lost everything in the fire. I mean, they're going to get the proceeds from the festival this weekend, but I'm sure they could use furniture too."

"That's a good question. A lot of it is pretty old, but maybe they'd like some of it."

Rose stepped outside for a moment to call Lizzie, Johnny Taylor's wife. Within ten minutes, Rose had found a home for most of the furniture. She went back inside to tell Jesse the good news.

"I'm glad I thought of the Taylors before you gave everything away," Rose said. "I'm hoping that and the money we make with the festival will get them on their feet again." She shoved her phone back in her pocket. "Now, where were we?"

Jesse handed her some garbage bags. "You were about to help me, otherwise I'll be here for the next month sorting this all out."

"I wouldn't mind that. It's nice having you here."

His dark eyes caught hers, and Rose resisted the urge to glance away.

"I can't stay," he said seriously. "You know that, right? Whether I sell this place or keep it, I would never live here."

Disappointment settled in. She'd known all along he was only here temporarily, but deep inside she realized she wanted him to stay. She'd missed him. She knew better than to let old feelings resurface, but some things just couldn't be helped. And it was a contradiction to everything she'd been telling herself…that she couldn't trust him again.

She played it off like it was no big deal. "Oh, I know. Honestly, I don't know why I said that. You've been clear you want nothing to do with this place." For good measure, she added, "Besides, I still hadn't forgiven you for leaving." She gave him a tight smile and went to work.

They took loads of trash to the farm's dumpster and loaded the medical equipment in the back of the truck with the last of the clothes.

Jesse closed the truck's tailgate with finality. "I think

that about does it for now. I'll run these to town and bring back the truck." He wiped his brow on his forearm.

"Actually, I need to pick up the dunking booth for the festival. Do you mind if I come along, and you can help me grab it on the way back?"

"I don't mind at all. Are you ready to go now?"

"Let me go to my apartment and fill up a water bottle to take. You want one?"

"That'd be perfect. Holler when you're ready. I'll be inside."

Rose watched Jesse for a moment as he went up the steps and back into the house. He'd always been on the thin side, but he had filled out over the years.

She forced herself to get moving. She ran up to her apartment and grabbed her things, plus the basket of eggs for Grammy. She texted Jesse on her way back down the stairs and met him at the truck.

"Why don't you drive?" she asked, walking around to the passenger side.

"Sounds good to me," he said.

"I thought we could drop off these eggs at Grammy's house too. It's on the way."

When they were settled in the truck, she handed him his water bottle, then put the basket of eggs in her lap. She'd ridden in this truck thousands of times, but it felt completely different with Jesse by her side. She flashbacked to them as young teens on a date. They truly hadn't had a clue about life back then. They'd been busy navigating the treacherous waters of high school, and then the anguish of Jesse losing his mom.

They'd been through a lot, but she preferred to remember the happier times.

Now if she could only get Jesse to think like that.

Nervously, she tucked a loose strand of hair behind one ear, then made herself relax against the worn-out leather seat.

After they pulled out on the main road, Rose showed Jesse how to get to Grammy's house a few miles away. When he parked, Jesse made no move to get out.

"Come in with me for a minute. Unlike me, I promise Grammy won't bite," Rose said.

Jesse laughed. "You said it, not me."

She smiled at him. "I know I can be a little difficult at times."

Jesse climbed out of the truck and stayed silent as he followed her up to the door. As they waited for Grammy to answer the doorbell, he asked, "Hey, do you think your grandma would want any of the medical equipment we're donating? Like the walker or the shower chair?"

Rose cut her eyes toward him. "If you value your life, do not mention it to her."

"Why? She might need them one day."

She shook her head. "Grammy doesn't consider herself old, and if you even suggest that she is, she'll give you an earful. Trust me, she's corrected me more than once."

"I think you're overreacting."

Just then, the door opened. "Rose," Grammy exclaimed like she hadn't seen her all year. She looked at Jesse. "And you. You're still here?" she asked, sounding surprised.

Rose glanced up at Jesse. This time, she was the one waggling her brows at him.

"Yes, ma'am," he said politely. "I'm still here."

"Hmm." Grammy studied him, then seemed to remember her manners. "Come on in, you two."

Rose and Jesse followed her through a hallway to the kitchen. "We can't stay long. I just wanted to bring you the fresh eggs I promised you." Rose handed her the basket.

"Thank you, sweetheart." Grammy took the basket and gestured toward the table. "Sit, have some iced tea with me."

"We really can't…" Rose started to say.

Jesse cut her off. "Iced tea sounds great," he said, taking a seat at the table.

Rose glared at him. This was supposed to be a quick stop. However, she went along with it and moved to a cabinet and started pulling out glasses while Grammy grabbed a pitcher of iced tea from the refrigerator.

"What are you up to today?" Grammy asked as she poured tea for the three of them.

"We're running errands, but later we have to keep setting up for the festival," Rose said. "What about you?"

"I've been cleaning, but later I have a date," she said with a grin.

"Really? With who?" Rose asked.

"His name is Bob. I met him the other day at water aerobics."

"So, it wasn't all old people after all," Jesse said.

"What?" Rose asked.

"That's what Grammy said the other day before she left for water aerobics. She hoped everyone there wasn't old."

"Well, they were all a bunch of old-timers, but Bob went out of his way to make me laugh, so I agreed to one date," Grammy said.

This wasn't too surprising. Grammy had a busy social life and went on dates every so often. The irony wasn't lost on Rose that her grandmother's dating life was more active than her own.

"If he makes the cut, why don't you bring him to the Sunflower Festival?" Rose said.

"We'll see," Grammy said idly.

Rose felt her phone vibrate in her pocket. It was a text from her mom that read, Saying goodbye to the canyon today. Here are a few pics for the road.

Rose scrolled through four pictures of her mom and dad at an overlook of the Grand Canyon. They looked tanned, healthy and happy. That made her smile.

"More pictures from my parents' road trip." Rose turned the phone so Grammy and Jesse could see.

"Beautiful view," Grammy said.

"Looks like they're having a great time," Jesse added.

"They're on their way back now." Rose shoved her phone back in her pocket. "We better get going. We have a lot of errands to run this afternoon."

They said goodbye to Grammy, but not before she gave Rose another bag of random things she didn't want anymore. Rose took the bag obediently. She'd learned long ago not to resist. Grammy always won.

Once back in the truck, Rose went through the bag. Brand-new pink slippers that were not Rose's size; a matching fuzzy robe that Rose would never wear; and a pair of generic sneakers with Velcro instead of shoe-laces. Rose shoved everything back in the bag.

"I told you, she always does this. Don't tell Grammy, but we'll drop this bag off at Goodwill, too."

Jesse laughed. "Come on, that pink robe looks just like you."

Rose tossed him a dirty look. "Careful. If you're here long enough, she'll start giving bags to you, too. Just ask Tony."

"Anything is better than 'are you still here?'" he mimicked Grammy's frequent question.

"That's what you get for leaving."

"I get an old lady's attitude?" he asked.

"Yep."

"Now I know where you get it from."

"Hey!" Rose playfully slapped his shoulder.

"While we're in town, can we drive past the old high school?" Jesse asked. "I haven't been back since I left."

"I haven't been back, either. I heard they put in a pool and built a new gym. While we're there, let's stop at the Sunlight Café and have lunch, then it'll really feel like old times."

"Is that place still around?" His voice held a hint of nostalgia. "Oh man, I loved their wings back in the day."

"It's still there. I go every now and then. Always loved their fries. They have that special seasoning sprinkled all over them."

"I remember."

"Do you do much cooking?" Rose asked suddenly. "You said you make spaghetti. Anything else?"

"I know my way around the kitchen."

"Really? What's your specialty?" she asked, glancing over at him.

"I guess my favorite thing is grilling. Does that count?" His dark eyes studied the road ahead.

"Grilling? I thought you said you lived in an apartment."

"I do. I'm on the second floor, and I have a private balcony. The grill's out there."

"That's the one thing we don't have on the farm. A grill. I wouldn't even know how to use one if I had it."

"It's pretty simple. You just turn on the gas, let it heat up for a few minutes and you're set. Occasionally you need to replace the gas, but that's easy enough."

"I'm sure you are oversimplifying it. What kind of things do you make?"

"Steak."

Rose chuckled. "Somehow I knew you would say that. What else?"

"Burgers, chicken, chops, fish… Pretty much anything you get from the meat or seafood counter. Sometimes I'll smoke pork butts and take them to the firehouse. The guys love that."

"Maybe we shouldn't be talking about food when I'm starving."

"No doubt. Now I'm in the mood for barbecue."

"Me, too. We can go to the Sunlight Café another time."

Ten minutes later, they dropped off their load at Goodwill, then with stomachs rumbling, they went in search of barbecue.

"You live around here, you should know where to go," Jesse said.

"I don't get out much. Maybe we don't have any barbecue places in town."

"It's the South, of course there's barbecue. Why don't you look it up on your phone?" Jesse asked as he drove down a random street.

"Oh, right." Rose pulled out her phone and asked Siri. Soon, they had two places to choose from.

They found the closest place a few streets over. Jesse pulled into the parking lot for a hole-in-the-wall barbecue joint. The overhead sign had a large cartoon pig wearing an apron and a chef's hat. Porky's Grill House flashed in bright red letters. The parking lot was packed for the lunch rush, a good sign. Jesse circled around looking for a spot, then gave up and parked across the street.

Jesse held the restaurant's door for Rose, and she stepped into a small dining room humming with chatter and clinking dishes. To their left was the kitchen, where a man stood at the edge of a massive oven, rotating large slabs of meat over a roaring fire. The delicious aroma of cooking meat assaulted her senses, and Rose found her mouth watering in anticipation.

A hostess led them to the last open booth. Jesse waited for Rose to sit, then sat down opposite her. The menu was a typical meat-and-two-sides affair. Everything looked delicious.

Jesse tilted his menu out of the way, saying, "Lunch is on me."

Rose glanced at him. "What? You don't have to, you know."

A sparkle entered his eyes, and his mouth curled up in an endearing little half smile that Rose knew was useless to resist. "I know," he said, "but you made me spaghetti last night. Plus, you helped me clean out the bedroom all morning. I owe you."

"I'm sure I'll need more help with the Sunflower Festival coming up."

"Then I'll gladly help you."

"We'll see about that. I was going to ask you to muck the stalls in the barn when we get back," she said.

"Were you? I suppose I might be able to help with that," he parried.

"Oh, and did I tell you, I need someone to help me try out the dunking booth?"

"I can do that, too. I've got a good arm." He held up an arm and flexed his biceps.

She gave him a devious little smile. "That's not what I mean, and you know it. I need someone to get in it and give it a whirl."

"I bet you do. I'm not promising anything."

Rose laughed. "You are easy to tease."

The waitress came over and set two glasses of water on the table. "Are you ready to order?"

"Sure. Rose, you want to go first?" Jesse asked.

"I'll take the pulled pork with slaw and beans and a glass of sweet tea," she said.

The waitress scribbled down the order, then turned to Jesse. "And you?"

"I'll take the ribs and beef brisket with the slaw and beans, as well. Sweet tea for me, too." When the waitress scurried away with their orders, Jesse leaned toward Rose. "Out of curiosity, who normally sits in the dunking booth?"

"This is the first year we've had it. I got it specifically for you." She smiled at him.

His eyes narrowed as if he was trying to figure out whether she was still teasing him.

Finally, she burst into laughter. "I'm joking. We have the dunking booth every year. Mostly folks from church volunteer to sit in it. The preacher is usually willing, and there are a few others I can count on. But by the end of the day, the kids take it over. It's a lot of fun."

Jesse playfully wiped his brow like he'd just escaped with his life. "And here I thought I would be stuck in it for the whole day."

"Don't worry, I'll need volunteers for the pie-throwing contest, too."

"When you say 'volunteers,' you actually mean someone who gets hit in the face with the pies?"

She gave him a big grin. "Now you're catching on. I always knew you had a brain in that pretty head of yours."

"Oh, I'm catching on, all right… Catching on to the fact you think you're funny."

"Or I'm getting even with you," she said lightly.

Jesse waggled his brows at her. "So you think I'm handsome, do you?"

"You're shameless."

"What do you mean?" he asked innocently.

"You know what I mean… You're a shameless flirt. You always have been."

"That's why you love me."

"I loved you once. Who says I still do?" she asked.

Jesse didn't have a quick rebuttal but sighed instead.

With his silence, Rose took the opportunity to ask something she'd been wondering. "So, you didn't tell me if you were dating anyone," she said, growing serious.

Jesse's brown eyes studied her. "Nobody right now."

"Right now? Does that mean you *were* dating someone?"

"There was someone for a few years. We were engaged and everything, but we broke up recently."

"If you don't mind me asking, why did you break it off?"

"It was mutual. We'd outgrown our relationship. We did more disagreeing than agreeing. We finally both realized we had gotten engaged because it'd seemed to be the next step, but we actually didn't make each other happy anymore. Being with somebody shouldn't be that hard. Neither one of us wanted a miserable marriage. Marriage is hard enough without starting off on the wrong foot."

"I'm sorry to hear that. Do you miss her?"

"This is terrible, but no, I don't miss her. Is that awful or what?"

"No, it sounds to me like you two did the right thing by calling it off."

"Yeah, we did. How about you? Are you dating anybody?"

Rose shifted uncomfortably now that she was in the hot seat. How could she answer this without sounding pathetic? "No. I don't have time for dating. Besides, there hasn't been anybody in a while that I've wanted to date."

"I find that hard to believe. I'm honestly surprised you aren't already happily married with a couple of kids."

"Maybe I would have been, if you'd stayed." She hadn't meant for that to slip out.

His brow lifted; she could tell she'd surprised him.

"I don't know what to say to that," he said.

"Sorry, but it's true. Don't you ever wonder where we'd be if you'd stayed in Eagletin?"

"You wouldn't have wanted me to stay. I wasn't the guy you needed me to be. I couldn't be around my father anymore."

"So, you've said. But haven't you ever wondered?"

"Yeah, sure I did. I also regretted leaving you, but I did what I had to."

"You could have done it differently. I would have gone with you if you'd asked." She hadn't planned to bring the past up again, but it'd been unavoidable.

"That wasn't an option. If you'd gone with me, you would have given up your dream school here. I couldn't let you give up your dream."

"It should have been my choice."

"Maybe you're right, but there is nothing I can do to change it now," Jesse said.

What could she say to that? He was right in that they couldn't turn back time and change things. Rose felt like they'd hit a stalemate. At that moment, the waitress dropped off their sweet tea and a basket of hot garlic bread. "Your lunch will be out in a couple of minutes," she said, then dashed off.

Rose grabbed a piece of garlic bread. "This smells yummy," she said as she tore the bread in two. They grew silent as they nibbled.

"Hey, you know what we should do?" Jesse asked, popping the last piece of bread in his mouth.

"What?" Rose asked.

"We should go for a dip in the lake for old times' sake."

Rose didn't know how to respond. It was probably the last thing she should do if she didn't want to get any more attached than she already was. But what if showing him how much fun it was to be back on the farm would convince him not to sell? Maybe he would have a change of heart. There were good memories there, too, and he could make new ones. With her.

"What?" Jesse said. "You have something against swimming on a hot day?"

"I don't know. I have a lot to do before the festival. And it's October, you know."

"It's also Florida, and it's ninety degrees outside. I think you can sneak away for an hour."

She shrugged, "I guess I could take a short break. Wait… Did you bring a suit?"

"I did."

"So, you planned this?"

"Maybe." He had the nerve to look sheepish.

He hadn't changed a bit. "Fine. We'll go swimming. But we are putting up the dunking booth first."

"Fine."

"And if you're going to get wet anyway, you can try it out."

"I'll pass," he said.

"Come on," she wheedled.

"Only if you try it out, too."

"We'll see."

The waitress brought their lunches, and Rose immediately dug into her pulled pork. Everything was delicious. She ate as much as she could, then pushed the plate away. "I'm stuffed."

"You're not going to finish that?" Jesse asked as he polished off the last of his beans, leaving an empty plate.

"There was too much. You can have the rest of mine."

"If you don't want it, sure, I'll take it." He pulled the plate over and finished it off. "Mmm, the pulled pork is good."

Rose remembered how they used to share food. It was like déjà vu all over again.

Jesse paid the bill, left a tip and headed out of Porky's with Rose. Lunch had been more fun than he anticipated. Rose was more fun than he anticipated, now that her temper had finally cooled off.

They walked back to the truck and Jesse started the engine. "Okay, where to?"

"The high school's not far from here. Let's go there."

"Sounds good." Jesse pulled out onto the street.

"Do you know where you're going?"

"Sure," he responded, though in truth he felt turned around. He used to know the streets of Eagletin, but he'd been gone so long that things had changed. His memory of the area had faded, too.

Rose was silent for a moment, then chimed in, "Um… we're going the wrong way. Unless you're taking the long way."

"The long way, of course." He shot her a quick smile, then changed direction.

Rose didn't say a thing.

Fifteen minutes later, they drove past the high school slowly. "It looks smaller, doesn't it?" Jesse asked.

"Yeah, it does. But it also looks the same."

"Do you want to get out and walk around?"

Rose looked out the window. "School's in session, so we better not. I'm pretty sure they don't want random people walking around campus."

"You're probably right."

Jesse drove around the block to view the other side of the school. In the large new pool, students with brightly colored caps and goggles swam while the PE teacher yelled from the sideline. The water rippled and sloshed over the sides.

Jesse rounded the corner and drove up the other side of the school. They came up to the new gym. Twice as big as the previous gym, and gleaming in the sun, it was hard to miss.

"Nice. The students here probably don't have a clue how good they have it."

"Nope. Not a clue," she said.

Jesse slowed the truck and pulled over in the grass to give them a good view of the school. "Man, we had so many good times here."

"I know."

"It makes you wonder what the old gang is up to," he said.

"Some of them are still around, others like you have moved on. You know, if you're still around Sunday, you should come to church. You can see some of the old gang there. Richie, Shea, Tyler, they all still go there. Richie and Shea are married now and have a baby."

"Really? I never knew they were an item."

"They weren't a couple in high school, but in the last five years, they started dating and got married. They're good for each other."

"Well, I'm glad they got their happy ending." Both Richie and Shea were good people; they deserved to be happy.

Someone should be happy, even if it wasn't him.

Oh, he was quite satisfied with his life. Being a firefighter was fulfilling, though lately he had started to wonder if it was something he wanted to do for the rest of his life. He had plenty of friends at work and dated some, even if he had struck out when it came to long-term relationships. Sometimes he just felt a little lost, like he was searching for something but couldn't figure out what.

He forced himself back to reality and glanced at

Rose to see if she was ready to drive on. But the words didn't come. He was struck by how beautiful she was. Her eyes were ice blue in the bright afternoon light. She wore little makeup but didn't really need any. Her face and arms were tan from working outside, and her usual ponytail suited her. Though she was small in stature, she had a big personality and could hold her own with the best of them.

When she caught him staring at her, she asked, "What's wrong? You're looking at me funny."

"It's nothing." Jesse turned away in embarrassment, as if she could read his mind. He cleared his throat, then started the truck.

Rose gave him directions to the party rental store where she'd rented the dunking booth. The thing was huge and took four people to load it. Luckily it fit in the bed of the truck and they could close the tail gate. When they got back to the farm, Tony and Justin helped Rose and Jesse get the booth out of the truck and set it up.

Jesse walked around the booth, inspecting it. Gently, he tugged the bull's-eye. It was attached to an arm that released the seat. The whole thing looked sturdy, but that didn't mean he wanted to be the one sitting in it. "So, are you adding the water now?" Jesse asked as he glanced around for the nearest hose.

"Nah. We'll wait till Thursday or Friday for that," Rose said.

"Then what was all that talk about me testing it for you?"

"Simple. I just wanted to scare you. You know, keep

you on your toes." She gave him a sugary-sweet smile and walked away.

Jesse watched her as she headed back to the barn, her sass radiating in each jaunty step. She'd sure had him going. He'd been ready to jump in the booth if she'd asked him nicely enough. How could he say no to her?

He thought about the ultimate decision he would have to make about the farm. Could he really sell it? Could he do that to Rose?

Did he want to keep the farm for himself? For the first time, it wasn't an outright no for Jesse.

He took a moment to survey his surroundings. The distant golden sunflower fields swayed in the afternoon breeze, their beauty truly stunning. Beyond the sunflowers were the citrus grove and the strawberry fields. He turned toward the barn and was reminded of all the animals that lived there. Betsy the cow, the horses, chickens and goats. What would become of them if he sold the farm? Would the new owners want them? Where would they go? Would Rose take them with her? How could she, when she had no place to go?

Guilt washed over Jesse. He didn't think he could do that to Rose or the other farm employees. Would it be right to let someone turn this one-of-a-kind farm into a housing or commercial development?

Rather than go back to the house and start cleaning out the next room, Jesse wanted to go after Rose. By the time he followed her into the barn, she had already started to unpack more decorations.

Rose glanced up at his footsteps. "So, you're here to help?" she asked.

"I'm here to steal you away for an hour."

One brow went up. "To do what?"

"Swimming at the lake. Let's cool off."

"If you're that hot, I can fill up the dunking booth after all," she said with a laugh.

"Very funny," he said dryly. "Come on. You can get away for a little while. I'm pretty sure there won't be a decoration emergency in the next hour."

"How do you know? This is the first year you've been around for the festival preparations. We have decoration emergencies all the time," she said, matter-of-factly.

Jesse walked over to Rose, took the armful of baskets she held and put them back in the box. She watched him silently, like she didn't know what to say.

He took her hand and gently pulled her toward the doors. "Come on. It won't kill you to have a few minutes of fun. If it puts you behind, I promise I'll help with the decorating."

"You promise?"

"Promise." He saw tension leave her face, and she smiled, flashing her even white teeth.

"Okay. But only for an hour, and then we come back."

"Got it. Now go change, and I'll meet you in five minutes. We can take the truck this time," he said.

She paused, then added, "Do you think we should invite the staff, too? I think they'd like the break."

Jesse hadn't planned on making it a party, but how could he say no to her? "Sure. The more the merrier."

"Great! I'll send them a text."

* * *

Rose sent off a text to the employees who were on the farm. There were only five of them on Wednesdays, three guys and two women. They were all going to think she'd lost her mind, or that it was a gag. They never took a break like this—a swim in the middle of the afternoon? With a big weekend coming up?

But wasn't that the best reason of all? They could all use a carefree hour to take a swim.

Rose ran up to her apartment to change. The thought of Jesse waiting on her made her feel like a nervous teen about to go on her first date. She rushed around, dropping everything she picked up.

What was wrong with her? She was a grown woman, not a lovesick teenager. She should stay and work on setting up the Sunflower Festival, not run off for a swim. But since she'd invited everyone else, that made it okay, didn't it? Too late to cancel now anyway.

Honestly, when was the last time she did something spontaneous? The sad truth was never. Jesse was always the fun one, and she'd always been serious. If he was only going to be here for a few days, what was the harm in enjoying his company?

She knew how to be careful. She could guard her heart. At least, that was what she told herself.

Rose changed into a one-piece swimsuit, pulled on some shorts and a tank top, slipped on flip-flops and grabbed two towels. She ran down the stairs before she did something stupid, like change her mind and go back to work. She was doing this, and she would have fun, she told herself. She deserved a break from all her work and her worries about this place.

Jesse waited in the cab of the truck with the engine running. She opened the door, and music poured out. It was a song from high school that she used to love, and all kinds of memories came flooding back.

Jesse saw her and turned down the volume. "Great song," he said, as if that explained why he'd turned it up so loud. "Did you text everyone?"

"Yep." Rose felt her pulse quicken as she climbed in next to him. She tried to ignore it.

"Are they coming?"

"I don't know." Which was the truth. No one had responded to her text.

Jesse took a shortcut to the lake. A cloud of dust followed the truck down the narrow path.

"You know, I used to go out to the lake all the time as a teenager just to get away from my dad," he said. "I haven't thought about this place in years. I think I've blocked it out, like everything else that had to do with the farm and my childhood."

He'd blocked her out, too, Rose thought.

The truck emerged into the clearing next to the lake. A couple of the farm guys were already doing cannonballs off the dock.

"Guess they saw your text," Jesse said dryly as he parked.

"I guess so," she said with a chuckle. "Why do I have a feeling this isn't the first time they've been out here?"

"Because it probably isn't."

"And why do I feel like there's not much more getting done today?"

Jesse smiled. "I can't imagine why you would say that."

They got out of the truck and strolled down the dock. Rose tossed a towel to Jesse, and he caught it easily with one hand. "Thanks," he drawled as he set it down at the end of the dock, then pulled off his shirt and slipped out of his shoes.

The two farmhands, Ricardo and Justin, were swimming around in deep water. Jesse had already met Justin, so Rose quickly introduced Jesse to Ricardo.

The guys immediately hooted and hollered for Jesse to throw Rose into the lake.

She shot them an indignant look. "Hey! Where's your loyalty?" She turned to Jesse, backing away. "Don't you dare, mister."

Jesse had the good sense to leave it alone. He held his hands up in surrender. "I would never," he said innocently.

Rose stiffened and waited until he'd moved past her on the dock. Not to be outdone by the other guys, Jesse took a running leap, pulled his knees to his chest and cannonballed into the lake. The splash covered everything within fifteen feet, just missing Rose.

Seconds later, Jesse surfaced in a rush, shook his wet head, and wiped his eyes. "Come on Rose, get in! The water's refreshing." His smile was infectious.

Unable to stop a grin, Rose pulled off her shorts but decided to leave her tank top on over the swimsuit. She put her hair up into a messy bun; there would be no cannonballs for her. Like a mature adult, she padded over to the ladder and slowly stepped down into the water. Her feet hit the bottom of the lake, and she bounced around on tiptoes until she faced Jesse.

"Ooh, this is colder than I expected," she said, biting her lip as she grew used to the temperature. The water reached her chest.

"It feels wonderful," Jesse said. He spread out his long arms and floated on his back next to her.

"I used to love swimming here in the summer," she said, squinting under the bright sun. "The lake used to feel like bath water, it was so warm."

"I can remember coming here and then getting in trouble because I wasn't doing my chores." Jesse sighed. "But it was worth every minute."

"You didn't always get in trouble. I think that's just what you've chosen to remember."

Jesse seemed thoughtful. The rumble of a UTV broke the peace of the lake. Tony drove up with the two other farm employees, Alexa and Susie. They all walked down to the end of the dock, various stages of amusement and disbelief on their faces.

"What is happening here?" Alexa called. "I told these guys there's no way Rose is giving us an afternoon off to swim. I had to come down here to see it for myself."

Rose laughed. "Not the whole afternoon. Just for an hour." She wondered if she would regret going along with Jesse's plans.

"We'll see," countered Jesse at her side.

Tony wasn't shy and jumped in the water.

"We don't have swimsuits," Susie said.

"Jump in anyway," Jesse said.

The two girls seemed to notice him for the first time, and interest showed on their faces. "And who are you?" asked Alexa.

Rose rolled her eyes. Jesse wasn't her boyfriend or anything, but that didn't mean she wanted to share him with Alexa or Susie. Trying hard to keep her voice indifferent, Rose answered. "That's right, you all haven't met. This is Jesse Cooper, Mr. Cooper's son. He owns the farm now."

That bit of news caught their attention. Their eyes went wide.

"Jesse, this is Alexa Johnson," Rose continued. "She's been with us for about two years now. She's my citrus expert and takes care of the citrus grove. And to her right is Susie Allen. She's been with us for almost a year. She helps me with a little bit of everything around the farm."

"Nice to meet you," the girls each said, almost in unison.

They decided not to go swimming but were happy to take off their shoes and dangle their feet over the edge of the dock. They chatted with Jesse for a few minutes while they watched everyone else swim.

"So, are you moving back to the farm?" Alexa asked. She'd never been shy. Susie, always the quieter one, was content to listen.

"No. I'm just here to clean out the house. I'll leave Monday after the festival."

"You're not going to live there? Seems like a perfectly good house going to waste."

Rose watched Jesse field the questions, all good

ones. She knew him well enough to know when he started to feel uncomfortable. He set his mouth in a straight line and the answers became shorter.

"Ah…no. No plans for anyone to live there," he said.

"Oh, that's a shame. Seems to me you should let Rose live there or rent it out. I'm sure people would pay big money to come live on a farm for a week."

Jesse immediately shot that down. "I won't do that. It's fine that the farm is open to the public, but we aren't going to have strangers staying overnight like a hotel." He politely excused himself to go swim a few laps.

Rose hated that she was aware of where he was the whole time as he swam. To distract herself, she swam over to Justin and Ricardo but left as soon as they started threatening to dunk her. She ended up going back to where the girls sat at the dock and chatted with them.

After a while, she got out of the water, grabbed her towel and sat on the brittle grass near the shore. It was just as dry near the lake as it was up at the farm. A soft breeze blew, and she was content to sit in the warm autumn sun while she dried off. Lazily, Rose laid back on the towel and closed her eyes, resting an arm across her face to block the sun. She heard her coworkers splashing in the distance, but other than that, all was quiet.

On the verge of falling asleep, Rose was startled when cold water dripped on her warm skin. Before she even opened her eyes, she knew it was Jesse because nobody else would dare. A deep chuckle confirmed it.

She sat straight up with a squeal. "What are you

doing?" Narrowing her eyes, she wiped the drops off her face. "I was half asleep," She scolded.

Jesse laughed it off as he threw his towel next to hers and plopped down on it. He shoved a hand in his wet hair and pushed it back, then gave her a lopsided smile. "Sorry." Teasingly, he leaned to one side and gently bumped shoulders with her. "You're about as prickly as a porcupine sometimes."

"You're right, maybe I am."

They were quiet for a minute, watching the others enjoy the lake. Eventually, Justin and Ricardo swam to the dock ladder and climbed out of the water. Alexa and Susie pulled their feet up, put their shoes back on and headed toward the UTV.

"This was fun! Thanks for inviting us," Tony called to Jesse and Rose as the girls loaded into the UTV. "We're heading back now."

Justin and Ricardo soon followed. They waved good-bye to Rose, then left on foot back to the farm.

With everyone gone, a hush settled over the lake. The afternoon sun was moving further west, a sign they'd been there for some time.

Rose realized she was reluctant to leave. "I wish we could stay right here forever. Don't you?" She stared out at the lake, but out of the corner of her eye she could see Jesse look at her. She felt herself blush but tried to act cool. She would not give him the satisfaction of knowing how much he affected her.

"I do, too."

She faced him. "You know, you're welcome to stay

here permanently." She kept her tone light, but she was dead serious.

"I know. Trust me, I know. And it's getting harder by the minute to leave. I never expected to have these feelings."

Was he talking about feelings for the farm or for her? She wasn't at all certain.

Keeping a level head, she reminded herself to treat him like a friend. "It's normal to have them. You grew up here. And if they're good feelings, maybe you can start visiting more often. Take an interest in the farm. If you don't want to live here, fine, but you can still be part of it."

"I know. I'm starting to see that now." He paused, like he was searching for words. Finally, he said, "Thank you for being so understanding."

"Well, sometimes I want to kick your butt if I'm being completely honest. But I also don't like kicking someone when they're already down. I know more than anyone what you've been through. You should be proud of yourself that you came out a stronger man for it."

"Thank you."

Rose stood and grabbed her towel. "You ready to head back? I can think of about a dozen things I need to do before I call it a day."

"Of course. If you're ready, then I'm ready," he said good-naturedly.

Rose offered a hand to help him up. Jesse smiled and let her pull him to his feet. When their fingers touched, it felt as intimate to Rose as if they'd kissed. She dropped his hand as soon as he was standing and headed toward the truck with him close behind.

How was she going to get through the rest of the week with him always around?

The more serious question: How would she handle it when he was gone again?

Chapter Six

Jesse steered the truck down the shady trail as he and Rose headed back. The afternoon sun tipped further west and beams of light shot through the tree canopy. Though his swimsuit was mostly dry, he sat on the thick towel anyway to protect the old leather seats. Rose had her towel snuggly wrapped around her waist. She sat next to him with her seat belt stretched over her lap, a contented look on her face. She seemed much more re-laxed now, like the swim did her some good.

"I was thinking about running back into town to get some groceries for the house," he said. "Why don't I make you dinner tonight? If you don't have other plans, that is?" His eyes darted back and forth from the road to Rose. Her cheeks were sun-kissed, and her hair was still pulled up on top of her head in a messy bun, with little tendrils of hair escaping everywhere.

"My only plans consist of unpacking decorations and putting up what I can before it's time to feed the animals and call it a night. Dinner sounds fabulous."

"Do you need anything from the store while I'm out?"

"Not the grocery store, but..." Rose checked her

watch. "It's almost four. Could you pick up the rest of the games and booths I rented from the party store? They're open until six. There are four more games I planned to get. They didn't fit in the truck with the dunking booth but you should be able to get them in one trip, it's nothing too heavy. It'll save me from having to go back to town tomorrow to get them."

"Sure, I can swing by and pick them up. Do you have any special requests for dinner?"

"Maybe something healthy, since we splurged for lunch."

"That's not quite what I meant." Jesse pulled up to the stairs to Rose's apartment, put the truck in Park and cut the engine.

Rose made no move to get out. Instead, she looked at him as if puzzled. "What did you mean?"

"Oh, I don't know. Like if you wanted steak, seafood or chicken. I don't think I'm in the mood for salad. I worked up an appetite with all that swimming."

Rose laughed. "A salad isn't the only healthy option. Have you ever heard of vegetables or lean meat? That kind of stuff. You know, be creative."

"Ah, got it. I'll figure something out and surprise you." He absently tapped his fingers on the steering wheel.

Rose climbed out of the truck, then turned back to face him in the cab. "You know, I don't have a grill. You'll be forced to use a stove," she teased.

"I think I can handle a stove."

"In that case, do you want to cook at my place?"

Jesse rubbed his jaw as he thought about it. For some

reason, he had the urge to make dinner at the farmhouse. "I think I want to make dinner in my old house. I haven't emptied out the kitchen yet, so I should be able to find what I need."

"Suit yourself. Don't forget to rinse off the layer of dust from everything."

He laughed out loud. "Come on, it adds flavor."

"I'll catch you later, smarty-pants. Don't forget to pick up my booths. Just text me when dinner's ready." She shut the passenger door before he could say anything, then ran up the stairs and disappeared into her apartment.

Jesse caught himself smiling after her. Rose had a way of bringing out the best in him. He'd missed that. It made him happy just being around her.

The women he'd dated over the years had never lived up to the high bar she'd set. There'd been times when he'd even wondered if his memories of her were accurate. Had he placed Rose on some pedestal, like she was the perfect girl? But being here with her again, he realized she was simply wonderful. They were good together.

The problem was, they weren't a couple. And that was all his fault, wasn't it? He could kick his younger self. But what good would that do? He'd done what he had to do to survive.

Jesse changed clothes back at the house, then headed to town, thoughts of Rose on his mind the whole time. He would need to make a decision about the property sale very soon, yet he was no closer to knowing what he wanted to do. Maybe he should just pass on the offer for now. But what if he didn't get another offer like it? Was he willing to let this chance pass by? What good was it to hang on to the farm if he had no intentions of ever working on it or living here?

Jesse had enjoyed his day with Rose, meeting the staff and the afternoon swim at the lake. What if every day could be like that?

After the house was cleaned out, maybe he could start fresh. His father was truly gone and couldn't hurt him anymore. Maybe it was time to let go of the pain and remember the better times, when his mother was alive and the three of them were a happy family. What if he could live here and start over with his own family?

When Jesse returned to the farm, he brought the groceries into the kitchen. In addition to ingredients for dinner, he'd bought a bag of apples to share with the horses. He took out two small ones and shoved them in the pockets of his khaki shorts. After the groceries were put away, he drove the truck to the barn and unloaded the games and booths that he'd picked up. Rose had been right; they were much more manageable than the dunking booth. One was a colorful fishing booth, another a ring toss, and the third was a mini golf green complete with balls and putters. The fourth was a painted wooden pumpkin and scarecrow stand where people could pose for pictures. He set everything inside the barn next to the remaining boxes of decorations.

Jesse half expected to see Rose in the barn and was disappointed when she wasn't there. He left the barn in search of her.

The sun sat low in the western sky, casting long

shadows over the empty corral. His gaze darted across the distant fields in search of Rose's familiar form. The horses nibbled on grass in a nearby pasture, so he took the five-minute stroll out to them to share the apples. It didn't take Missy any coaxing. She trotted over and greeted Jesse like they were old friends. She was already his favorite.

"Here you go, old girl. A special treat for you, just like I promised." He pulled out one of the apples and held it out to her on a flat hand. In a couple horse-size chomps, the apple disappeared.

When Moe saw him feeding Missy, he walked up and gently nudged Jesse's shoulder.

"Don't worry, I'm not leaving you out." Pulling out the second apple, Jesse offered it to Moe. He stroked the gelding's neck as he gobbled up the apple.

From there, Jesse walked over to the goat pen. Amused at their bleats of welcome, he slipped through the gate and took a few minutes to pet the friendly goats.

"I'm sorry I didn't bring you anything, but Rose will be here soon with your supper."

A little white goat bleated as if in complaint.

"You talking to goats now?" Rose asked from behind, startling Jesse. A little thrill shot through him.

He stood and turned toward her. "I rather like talking to goats, they don't talk back."

Rose had changed back into jeans and a T-shirt and she held a bin full of hay for the goats. "I don't know if I should take your answer personally or not."

"Just teasing. You want some help?"

"That would be nice. Thanks."

Jesse opened the gate for her and helped her pass out the hay to the goats.

"So, did you just get back?" she asked.

"A few minutes ago. I put the games and booths inside the barn. Will those be enough for the festival?"

"We have more coming on Thursday from the church."

"That's good." Jesse threw down some hay, then grabbed another handful. "Dinner shouldn't take long."

"I'm almost finished with my chores. I just need to get the horses in and then clean up a little."

"How about you come over in an hour? Would that work?"

"Perfect. Should I bring anything?"

"I don't think so. I've got everything covered. But thanks."

When they finished feeding the goats, Jesse went back to the main house and started dinner. He didn't know if Rose would think a rice pilaf was healthy, but he figured he'd get a gold star for the salmon and asparagus at least.

Right on time, Rose rang the doorbell. When Jesse answered the door, he wasn't prepared for what he saw. Yes, Rose was always beautiful, but tonight she took his breath away. She wore her hair down and straight. It was a shiny, golden honey-brown color. She wore jeans with a blue blouse that brought out her light blue eyes. Her cheeks were pinker than usual thanks to her sunburn.

Jesse had to mentally shake himself. "Hey there. Good timing. Come on in." He tried to be smooth but feared she knew him well enough to know he was the same goofball he'd always been.

"Thanks. Is dinner ready?" She walked past him with a covered plate in her hand.

"Just about. I was waiting for you to get here before I threw on the fish."

She turned back to face him. "Fish? That sounds healthy."

"I hope you like salmon."

"I love it." She handed him the plate. "Here, this is for dessert."

Jesse lifted the aluminum foil and inhaled the smell of fresh chocolate chip cookies. "You didn't have to bring anything, but I'm so glad you did."

"I couldn't come empty-handed," she said, grinning.

"When did you have time to make these?"

"It's nothing. They were slice-and-bake. Cookie dough is like milk and eggs. I always have some on hand."

"Well, thank you. Come in, make yourself at home." Jesse led Rose into the kitchen and set the cookies down on the table. On the stove, a hot skillet waited. Jesse started the salmon. "These only take a few minutes. Go ahead and grab yourself something to drink out of the fridge."

Rose pulled out a pitcher of lemonade, grabbed a glass from the dish rack on the counter and poured herself a drink. "I'm impressed. You already have the table set and everything," she said, putting the pitcher back in the refrigerator.

"Oh ye of little faith. I told you I would make dinner," he said.

"Is there anything I can do?"

"Nope, I have it handled. Just relax. I know it's been a long day."

She scratched her head and looked around the kitchen as if she wasn't sure what to do with herself. "I'm not used to relaxing. I normally go nonstop until I conk out at night. There are always so many chores that need to get done."

Jesse flipped the salmon, then glanced at her. "Do you need more help around here?"

"If you mean, should I hire more people, the answer is no. But if you're asking whether I could use your help around here, the answer is yes."

She looked hopeful, and it broke his heart in a way he had not expected. Even though he was starting to not hate the farm anymore, he didn't want to commit to anything. All of this was new for him and unexpected.

"I can't promise to help any more after this week," he said slowly. "I've been clear about not staying. This is about closure for me."

"I know. But a girl can dream, can't she?" She went over to the table and sat down.

Jesse plated the warm rice and asparagus, then added the salmon at the last second. He carried the two plates to the table.

Rose rewarded him with an appreciative smile. "This looks delicious. Thank you."

"You're welcome. Anytime." Jesse took a seat across from her, where he'd always sat growing up. Old habits were hard to break. It didn't feel right sitting in his mom's or dad's spot at either end of the table.

Rose paused with her fork in midair. "This is really good. It definitely exceeded my expectations."

Jesse laughed. "Thanks. I'm glad you're not disappointed."

"Now that I know you can cook, I won't be feeling sorry for you anymore or imagining you over here hungry."

"I guess I just ruined my chance for more sympathy spaghetti, didn't I?"

Rose ate some of the asparagus, then asked, "So, is this your smooth move for the ladies? Cooking for them?"

Jesse shook his head at the question. "What? Why would you say that?"

"I'm just wondering if this is the meal you make for all your dates."

"You think this is a date?"

"No, that's not what I meant," Rose said in a rush. Her pink cheeks turned pinker.

She was adorable.

But he realized she wasn't wrong about dinner. "Okay, I may have to confess something to you. I have made this dinner for a date or two. But I promise you, this is not some elaborate plan to make a move. It just happens to be in the rotation of about a handful of things I can make that turn out good."

Through narrowed eyes, Rose studied him. Finally, she laughed. "Okay, I believe you. And I can't wait to try what else is in the rotation."

"Good, because it's in the fridge all ready for tomorrow night."

She raised her brows. "And what is that?"

"Don't you want to be surprised?"

"Not at all. Spill it."

"Well, I make the best homemade chicken Marsala."

"Ooh, that sounds yummy." She took a sip of her lemonade, then turned thoughtful. "Can I tell you something?"

Jesse set his fork down and sat up straighter, ready for whatever it was she had to say. "Of course. You can say anything to me."

"It's been weird having you around the farm. When I first saw you Saturday, I recognized you, but you were more like a stranger to me. Do you know what I mean? You'd been gone for so long, I realized that I didn't know you anymore. But after spending the last couple of days with you, I realize you're still the same guy I knew back when we were kids. I feel like I blinked, and you're here again. That fun-loving, sweet guy I knew is here again. Teasing me, flirting with me, finishing my plate at lunch, just like old times."

"I know what you mean. I have to say, I dreaded coming back home. I could only think about how hard it would be to face my dad's memory. But that's only been a small part of this homecoming. Having you here and remembering how good we were together has been unexpected. It's been good for me, too."

"But yet, you don't want to stay?"

Jesse didn't know how to answer that. If he did sell, it would ruin everything with Rose. "Give me time. I'm figuring it out as I go. Can we enjoy tonight, though?"

"Sure," she said. However, her whole body stiffened as she went back to her dinner.

Jesse took a bite of salmon. "You know, I was thinking about your rose garden. Do you advertise it like you do the sunflowers?"

"No. Folks usually stumble on it when they finish with the gardening classes on Saturdays. It's nice and all, but the sunflowers are our bread-and-butter."

"I don't think you give yourself enough credit. That rose garden is stunning. We should be advertising it along with the other things like the classes, the sunflowers, the strawberry picking. It can all be part of the experience."

She looked at him funny.

"What?" he asked. Did he have food on his chin or something? He wiped his mouth with a napkin.

"You said 'we.' *We* should be advertising it."

"Oh, well…you know what I meant. *You* should be advertising it."

"I'll have to think about it," she said. "We already have thousands of brochures printed up, and it'd cost money to make any big changes to the website. I would have to think of an angle and figure out what would attract people the most."

"The way I see it, you've already done all the hard work by creating the garden. Now you just have to promote it. The next time you print the brochures, think about adding it."

"I guess so." She didn't seem too convinced.

How could she not see how amazing it was? Jesse decided to change the subject to something she was more comfortable with. "I've been thinking about joining you at church this Sunday. It'll be good to see everyone again. I can't remember the last time I attended services."

"Before college?"

"Pretty much." He started in on the rice.

"I think that's great. It'll give you a chance to see some old friends. So, you go back to work Monday?"

"Yeah. I kind of dread it."

"Why?" she asked, leaning back as if to study him.

Jesse shrugged. "It's nice to be on vacation, even though this isn't a real vacation."

"Ah. You're going to miss me. I knew it."

Jesse laughed. "That, too."

"Seriously, though, you don't like your job?" Rose asked. She took a final bite of salmon, then pushed her plate away.

"I like being a firefighter," Jesse said thoughtfully. "The first couple of years I loved it. It was my dream job. Every boy wants to be a firefighter when they grow up, right? I've made some great friends, and I've learned a lot, but lately I've been thinking about moving on. It's hard to explain, but sometimes I feel like there should be more in my life than just work."

"Maybe your soul's secretly yearning to be a farmer," she said with a grin.

Jesse laughed. "Yearning? I don't think I'm yearning to do anything."

"I think it's a sign from God that it's time to come home," Rose said lightly as she reached for the cookies.

"And this is my home?"

"Of course, this is home. Don't you see, this farm is wonderful. I love this place."

"My dad should have left it to you then."

"I wish he had. Then I wouldn't be worried about you selling it."

Jesse looked away, suddenly uncomfortable.

She grew serious. "If you have any affection for me, I am begging you to hang on to this place. Let me run it. You won't have to do a thing. Please don't sell the farm."

"As much as I would love to make you happy, I can't keep this place just for you. I originally had no plans to keep it, and yes, I've been wavering over this decision. But if I keep it, it has to be my decision."

He thought he saw her eyes water, but she was so stubborn she didn't let any tears slide down her cheeks. Instead she blinked a few times. He knew she would refuse to cry in front of him.

"I think I better go now," she said.

"Please don't go away mad."

"I'm not," she snapped. "It's just time to go home and get some sleep. I'm exhausted. Dawn comes real fast when you live on a farm. But you wouldn't know anything about that, would you?"

He widened his eyes at her tone. "I think I can remember what it's like to get up at dawn to work in the fields. To come home from school and have a list of chores a mile long. I grew up here, remember?"

"I thought you'd forgotten all that. It's why you ran away at eighteen, isn't it? To forget?"

"I ran away to escape my father. Not the farm itself."

"Well, he's gone now. Maybe it's time you came home for good."

Jesse didn't want to argue with her. Rose had been the best part of his week. He didn't want to make her mad or hurt her. He hated to admit it, but she might be right. Could the farm be part of his life?

Rose pushed her chair back and stood up. The mood had been ruined, and she was clearly set on leaving. Jesse stood as well.

"I'll leave the rest of the cookies here for you," she offered.

"Thanks," he said awkwardly. He followed her to the front door.

"Thank you again for dinner. It was really good."

Jesse held the door open, not quite ready to let her go. There was a time he would have been comfortable enough to lean in for a kiss, but that was long ago. If he were to try something like that right now, she'd reject him after the tension of the last ten minutes. They needed to keep things friendly anyway. His visit was just that. A visit. He'd be leaving Monday morning.

"Good night," he said at last.

"Good night." Rose gave him a tight smile. He could see the resignation on her face as she left.

Jesse watched her walk away into the night, the short trip back to her apartment. The evening had been kind of strange. He and Rose had this push and pull when they were around one another. One minute they were keeping each other at arm's length and the next they were drawn to one another. He had the impression she felt the same way. It was confusing and he wasn't quite sure what to do about it.

Jesse was starting to wonder what it would be like to be on the farm more. Not necessarily move back but visit more. Of course, that would mean keeping it.

Jesse shook his head. He wasn't sure what he wanted.

Chapter Seven

The next morning, Jesse rose early. It was already Thursday, and he needed to get as much done as possible before the Sunflower Festival started on Friday. First, he wanted to check the irrigation system because watering the sunflower fields by hand was a lot of work. How did Rose keep up with it?

Jesse grabbed a toolbox and shovel on his way out. After a couple hours of troubleshooting, he thought he knew what the problem was; it was something his dad had shown him long ago. Jesse headed to town for the hardware store, bought the supplies he needed and went back to make the repairs. As he tested the irrigation system, he said a little prayer that it would work. When the old system roared to life, Jesse practically danced with joy. He couldn't wait to surprise Rose with the news.

For the time being, he went back to the house to continue Operation Cleanout. Jesse went through each room in the house, emptying drawers and clearing off surfaces. He ended up throwing a lot of stuff away, but did come across a small jewelry box hidden in the dresser. Lifting the lid, he found his parents wedding rings along with his mom's diamond engagement ring.

He recalled his mother saying the engagement ring was passed down from his grandmother. There was other jewelry in the box, but Jesse felt like the rings were the real treasure. He closed the lid and moved the box to his room for safe keeping.

Jesse finished his parents' bedroom and moved on to his father's office. Emptying his father's desk, he stumbled on some old news clippings from his high school football days. Surprised, Jesse sat back in the office chair and skimmed through the articles. Why would his dad save these? He'd never cared about Jesse's games or anything else he did after his mother was gone. At least that was what he'd always thought.

Jesse pushed away from the desk, leaving the clippings behind, and walked out. He had to get away from the house and everything it represented. He needed time to absorb…to think.

Automatically he went in search of Rose, the one person who would understand what it all meant. She'd been back in his life for less than a week, and she was already the most important person he knew. He needed to share with her what he'd found.

His long legs carried him to the barnyard. The booths and games he'd picked up the day before had been set up that morning, and the place looked festive with the lights and decorations. He found Rose in the garden, on her hands and knees pulling weeds. She jumped when he reached her.

"Jesse! You startled me," Rose said. She straightened and wiped her brow with the back of her hand.

"I'm sorry. I just had to talk to somebody." Jesse stood over her with his hands on his hips.

She squinted up at him against the bright sun. "Why? What's wrong?"

"Everything's okay," he promised. "It's just I found something today, and I'm not sure what to think about it."

"Come on, let's go sit in the shade. Tell me what you found." Rose led him to a bench under a row of arches covered in rose vines. The space was shady and the scent of roses hung thick in the air. "What's going on?" she asked, her voice filled with concern as she waited for his answer.

Jesse propped his elbows on his knees and clasped his hands. "Today, when I cleaned out my dad's desk, I ran across some newspaper clippings that he saved from when I was in high school. They were articles from the local paper about the football team. They had my name and picture in them."

"You always were one of the best players on the team, and you made it to the playoffs. It's not surprising you were in the paper."

"It's not that. It's the fact that he saved them. To my face, he barely acknowledged I was even on the football team. He never asked me how it was going, and he never went to any games. I honestly thought he didn't care about it at all. So why would he save the articles?"

"Because he did care about you."

"He didn't act like it. He barely talked to me. It was like two strangers living together, coexisting. Not a parent and their only child. When he did talk to me, he was mean and angry. I never could do anything right in his eyes, and he made sure I knew it."

Rose shook her head. "I'm sorry. I know it was hard." She rubbed his back in comfort.

"He was really angry with me after the car accident. He blamed me for my mother's death. I blamed myself." Jesse squeezed his eyes shut. "You know, I lived with him for almost three years after my mom was gone, and it never got better. Why didn't he ever tell me he was following my games? It would have meant the world to me."

"I don't know for sure, but maybe he didn't know how to express himself. Some people are no good at saying the right thing. Add in the fact he was still grieving for your mom."

Jesse scrubbed his hand across his face in frustration. This went against everything he'd believed. He'd always thought of his father as the villain.

Rose continued, "After you were gone, I got to know him. I think he hit rock bottom, being left alone. He lost your mother, and then you left him. After a while, he started to go to church. We were all a little shocked to see him there. I really think it took him finding God for him to change. He became a better man, like he found an inner peace."

"I haven't told you this," Jesse said slowly, "but he left me a phone message once. It was just a few years after I left home. He said he was sorry and asked me to call him or come see him. I was still so angry with him that I never did. I deleted the message and forgot all about it."

"You have to believe he loved you. I know he had an awful way of showing it when you were a teenage boy, but he loved you." Rose reached over and squeezed his hand.

Just then, Alexa walked up to them. "Hey, Rose," she said. "Pastor Ronnie is here along with a bunch of other folks. They're looking for you."

"Thanks. They're here to help me finish setting up for the festival. I'll be right there."

Alexa nodded. "I'll let them know you're coming." She left them alone once again in the garden.

Rose glanced at Jesse. "Are you going to be okay?"

"Yeah, I'll be fine. I was just shocked and had to tell somebody or explode."

"Why don't you come with me to say hello to Pastor Ronnie? I know he would love to see you after all these years."

Jesse followed Rose out of the garden, then remembered the good news. "Oh, I looked at the irrigation system and figured out the problem. I was able to get it going."

Rose stopped in her tracks, "You were able to get it working? How? I was told by the company I called that we needed to replace it. They said they couldn't fix it."

Jesse scratched his chin. "Hmm. Sounds to me like they were trying to sell you an irrigation system."

Annoyance flashed across her face. "Maybe you're right. They'd make more money installing a new one over repairing the old one. I told you it was pricey. I feel like such a sucker."

"Don't blame yourself. How would you know otherwise?"

Rose started walking again, her arms across her chest and her eyes studying the ground. She was either deep in thought or upset.

"Hey, the important thing is that the irrigation system works, right?" he pointed out. "No more hand watering."

She squinted up at him. "You're right, but it's frustrating. We've worked our fingers to the bone watering this place for months. I wish you'd come back sooner."

Jesse didn't respond to that, but inside, he was starting to feel the same way.

When they reached the barnyard, the volunteers milled around as they waited for Rose. Two trucks in the parking lot held more games and booths.

Jesse recognized his old pastor immediately. Salt-and-pepper hair had been replaced with a head full of white hair, and there seemed to be more wrinkles than before. A large grin split Pastor Ronnie's face when he saw Jesse, and he thrust a hand out to greet him. "Jesse Cooper. Welcome back. You have been missed, son." His deep voice was full of emotion, like he meant it.

Jesse shook his hand, genuinely happy to see him. "Thank you, sir. I've missed you all, too."

An older couple next to Pastor Ronnie turned toward Jesse, and he recognized the Dawkinses instantly. Their smiles were huge as Mr. Dawkins shook Jesse's hand and Mrs. Dawkins gave him a hug.

She stepped back and gave him a once-over. "Jesse Cooper, you are all grown up and handsome as can be."

Jesse shook off the compliment. "Good to see you, Mrs. Dawkins. It's been ages."

Two young men walked over, and Jesse recognized one of them as his old friend Tyler from high school. Back then, they'd gone to the same church and were pretty tight. After Jesse left for college, they'd lost touch.

Tyler smiled when he recognized Jesse. "Hey, man. I can't believe it's you."

"Yeah, good to see you."

They gave each other a brief brotherly hug.

Remembering his manners, Tyler introduced a friend standing next to him as Robert. A young woman joined them, and Tyler threw his arm over her shoulder. "This is my fiancée, Kim. I don't know if you two remember each other. She went to our high school, but she was a couple years behind us."

"Nice to meet you. I've heard lots of stories about you," Kim said.

"Nothing too awful, I hope." Jesse was only half joking.

"No, no. All good," she reassured him. "Thank you for letting us have the festival on the farm. This year it's for a cause that hits close to home. Our friends Johnny and Lizzie Taylor."

"I'm glad we can help them. Though this is all Rose's doing."

"Isn't she so great?" Kim added. "We just love Rose."

Jesse hid a proud smile.

Just then, Rose called for all the volunteers to gather so she could assign them their duties. Everyone joined except for Pastor Ronnie and Jesse, who hung back to keep catching up.

"How long has it been since you've visited?" Pastor Ronnie asked. They were the same height, but the pastor was a large man and probably had a hundred pounds on Jesse.

"Ten years. I left right after high school."

"Seems like only yesterday you were a little boy hanging onto your sweet mama's skirt."

Jesse's heart warmed. "I think I remember that."

"You know, we've missed your mother and your father."

Jesse didn't want to be rude and held his tongue about his father. He still found it hard to have anything good to say. He managed to croak out a thank-you.

If Ronnie noticed he was uncomfortable, he did not let on. "Are you here to help with the Sunflower Festival this year?"

"I actually came back to clean out my parents' house. It just so happens the festival is at the same time, so I've kind of been recruited to help."

"Good timing. The festival is a lot of fun every year. We all look forward to it. I'm sure Rose is happy to have you back."

"Let's just say she was a little surprised to see me, but after getting over her initial shock, she's been great."

"Isn't there some history between you two?" Pastor Ronnie asked, his arms folded over his chest.

Jesse's eyes landed on Rose, organizing volunteers across the barnyard. "You have a good memory. We dated in high school, but that was a long time ago."

"That's what I thought. She's a good girl. I've watched her grow up and take over this farm. When your dad grew too sick to take care of himself, she took care of him, too. Any man would be lucky to have her as his wife."

Jesse wasn't much in the mood to talk about his dating life with his old pastor. "You're right," he agreed politely. "Any man would be lucky to have her."

As if she'd heard him, Rose caught his eye and smiled at Jesse. He nodded in her direction. A minute later, she walked up to them. "I have a job for you two, if you're up to it, Pastor," she said. "I need you to take our Sunflower Festival sign and hang it at the entrance. You'll need the ladder. And you can carry it down there on the truck."

As Jesse and the pastor drove down to the farm's entrance and hung the twenty-foot sign, Jesse told him about college and becoming a firefighter.

"None of us have seen you in so long. Did you stay away because of your father?" the pastor asked as they drove back to the barnyard.

Jesse parked the truck but left it running as they talked. "I did. We weren't close… He didn't make things easy for me after my mom passed away. I left as soon as I could and never wanted to come back while he was still here." That was way more information than he'd planned to share, but the pastor had a way about him that made a person want to tell him everything.

Pastor Ronnie looked at him with understanding in his eyes. "I am sorry, son, for what you've been through. Life is not always fair. To lose a loving parent at such a young age, it couldn't have been easy for you."

"When my mom died, I pretty much lost two parents. My dad was so heartbroken over her loss that he barely spoke to me, and he was so angry when he did. You see, he blamed me for the accident."

"What if I told you he regretted how he treated you? After you left, he started attending church. It took you leaving for him to realize how alone he was. One day he came to visit me. I tell you what, all I saw was a broken man." The pastor shook his head. "He had so much regret and guilt when it came to you. How he treated you, how he wasn't there for you. He regretted it all."

Jesse studied the pastor. Rose had tried to tell him his dad had changed, but he hadn't been ready to accept it. Was he finally open to hearing about his father's regret?

The pastor continued, "I told him that if he was truly sorry, God would forgive him, but he had to forgive himself, too." Pastor Ronnie paused and looked Jesse straight in the eye. "Today, I want to say something to you. I think that you're carrying around those old hurt feelings toward your father. Don't you think it's time that you forgive him? Let go of that pain?"

Jesse didn't know what to say. They sat in the truck in silence, the AC humming. He stared down at his hands gripping the steering wheel. Pastor Ronnie had hit the nail on the head. How could he have known?

The pastor patted Jesse's shoulder. "That's all I'm going to say for now. You come find me if you have any questions or if you want to talk some more."

Jesse nodded. "Thank you, Pastor. It's a lot for me

to think about. I appreciate you taking the time to tell me, though."

"If you're going to be around for a while, why don't you come to church on Sunday? Everybody would love to see you again."

Jesse smiled. "Rose is already twisting my arm to come. I plan on visiting this Sunday."

The pastor gave him a warm look. "Don't you know, it's not visiting when it's the church you grew up in... It's coming home."

Chapter Eight

Toward the end of the afternoon, the last of the church volunteers left. Rose meandered through the rows of games and booths lined up in an open grassy field, a short distance from the picnic tables and where the food trucks were going to be. Everything had been hung, decorated and staged for the long festival weekend. Jesse had helped with the setup all afternoon. Rose had noticed that he recognized a couple of the church volunteers and met a few new ones, as well. Everyone was so friendly and willing to help, she hoped it made him miss the sense of community of a small town. Would it make him miss the farm enough not to sell it? Perhaps make him want to return on a more permanent basis?

Rose hadn't had a chance to talk to him anymore about his dad, and maybe that was for the best. He needed time to think.

She hated that the week with Jesse was almost over. It had flown by. She'd grown attached to him again, practically over night, but was the feeling mutual? She had a feeling that it was, but she couldn't be sure. He'd made it clear he didn't want anything to do with the farm, and there was still a good chance he would sell it.

Deep down, Rose knew she should be careful with her heart. Jesse had left her once to get away from his father and the farm. If history had taught her anything, he could leave again. She needed to be prepared. Could she really trust him?

Jesse stood at the dunking booth with a hose, filling it with water. Rose walked over to him.

"Hey there. Is the tank almost full?" She stopped next to him and peeked in. The water was close to the fill line.

"Yeah, I'm about to shut it off." Jesse rested his arms on the edge of the tank as he watched the water slowly rise.

"I was about to take a ride to the sunflower fields and pick some fresh blossoms for tomorrow," she said. "A lot of folks pick their own, but others will wait and buy them as they're leaving. Do you mind helping me? It'll go faster with two people."

"Sure. Let me just shut off the water, and I'll join you."

"I'll swing by and get you." Rose grabbed the UTV from the barn and picked Jesse up near the hose spigot. "Hold on," she said, then hit the gas pedal.

Jesse grabbed hold of the vehicle's frame just in time. "A little more warning next time, would ya?"

"Come on. How long have we known each other? I think by now you'd know how I drive."

Jesse laughed. Rose picked up speed, the wind whipping past them as the motor roared. It felt good to sit down after being on her feet all day, but it was also a preview of the long weekend to come. Rose reached the front of the sunflower fields but kept going toward the back pastures.

"Where are you going?" Jesse asked over the noise of the engine. "I thought we were picking sunflowers."

"We are. But the fields closest to the barn and parking lot will get the most foot traffic this weekend. We're going to pick flowers at the opposite end, where visitors won't go."

"Smart. I never would have thought of that."

"Sure you would. Hang around here long enough, you'll figure it all out again."

"I don't know about that. A lot has changed since I left."

"Yes, but there's a lot that's the same."

Jesse was quiet for a minute, then said, "It was nice to see Pastor Ronnie and Tyler today. I've missed them."

"Don't forget the Dawkins, too. They're such a sweet couple. They helped me care for your dad toward the end. They would take turns and come over to sit with him during the day while I was busy dealing with the farm. Then at night, I'd stay with him."

Rose expected him to change the subject, but instead he seemed to absorb the information.

He scrubbed his face with one hand, then sighed heavily. "You did so much for him. How long was it like that, someone having to care for him twenty-four hours a day?"

"Two months."

Rose reached the back of the sunflower field and drove through two long rows of blossoms as golden as miniature suns. Eventually, she stopped in the middle of the field with nothing but sunflowers around them, radiant with the sunset light. The irrigation system had only been running a day, and already the flowers seemed perkier.

Rose said a silent thank-you to God because she knew it was an answer to prayer. She cut the engine, and nature's silence surrounded them. She stared out at the ocean of sunflowers, not really seeing them. Was Jesse finally ready to hear about his dad?

"Your dad fought lung cancer for a year. He went to chemo treatments on his own and took care of himself as long as he could. I checked in on him periodically and helped with things like shopping, picking up his meds, cooking, housework, bills and taking care of the farm. He managed on his own for a while like that, and I thought things would get better. But then he went downhill practically overnight. The last two months, he was too sick to take care of himself. Mr. and Mrs. Dawkins started helping me during the day while I worked the farm, and then I took care of him at night. In his final two weeks we had hospice coming out. The hospice nurses would visit regularly to check on him and make sure he was comfortable, but they didn't stay. It was up to us to care for him." She turned to face Jesse.

He met her stare with sad eyes. "I'm sorry I put you in that situation."

"You didn't put me in that situation, I did. I was your dad's friend. He needed help, and I helped him. I'd do it again. I'm not telling you all this to make you feel bad, Jesse. I'm telling you so you know what your dad's last year was like. Whether you hate him or not, he was still your father. You should know what happened."

"You're right."

"Of course I'm right. I'm always right. When are you going to learn this?" she joked, attempting to ease the tension.

Jesse laughed. "You're impossible." He reached over and pretend to ruffle her hair.

Rose ducked away. "Be nice, because this impossible girl is your ride back. Now, come on, let's cut some flowers before we lose what's left of daylight."

She'd brought a couple pairs of shears and several large bins to fill with flowers. "When you cut the flowers, leave the stems a couple of feet long."

"Yes, ma'am. I've cut sunflowers before. I remember," Jesse said, matter-of-factly.

Rose smiled at him as she handed over a pair of shears. "Forgive me. I'm used to bossing everyone around, or nothing would get done right around here."

"No apologies needed. You've done a great job with everything. No complaints from me."

"Thank you. Now, come on," she said.

Working side by side, they quickly filled the bins with big sunflower heads on long stalks, their large brown centers full of seeds.

"I remember picking sunflowers with my mom," Jesse said. He placed another flower in an already full bin, its petals glittering with drops of water from a recent soaking. "We sold most of them to florists, but we did keep the imperfect ones. We'd let them mature so we could harvest the seeds. My mom would give away goody bags full of seeds to her friends and family. She was known for it, and people would always ask us for them. I think she liked blessing others."

Rose paused to join him in the memory. "I remember her handing out the bags at church. She gave one to my mom and dad. I was just a kid, and I thought it was the best thing in the world."

"What do you do with extra seeds now?"

She laughed. "What do you think? We sell them in the store. I told you, we had to get creative to make money any way we could."

"Smart. I think you did the right thing."

"We sell all sorts of stuff besides the seeds. Did you meet Lolly last weekend?"

Jesse nodded.

"Lolly is a rock star when it comes to canning and jarring what we grow. I give her free rein, and she makes whatever's in season that she's in the mood for. Everything from strawberry jam to pickles to orange marmalade to jalapeño jelly."

Jesse made a face at the last menu item.

Rose laughed. "Don't knock it until you try it. Jalapeño jelly is better than it sounds. Add a little cream cheese and put it on a cracker…" She paused to rub her belly. "Yummy."

"I'll take your word for it." Jesse looked doubtful as he snipped another stem. "What else have you changed around here to make money?"

Rose thought for a minute. "We tried breeding the goats and chickens to sell, but I never had the heart to let any of them go. I probably doomed myself when I started naming the babies. I just got too attached."

"You always were a softy."

"That's what your dad said, too."

Jesse noticeably stiffened.

"I'm sorry. I wasn't trying to bring him up again."

"It's okay. I need to stop being sensitive."

Rose liked having Jesse working at her side. He'd been a downright hero, first helping clear that tree, then fixing the fence, then repairing the irrigation system. She really could get used to having him around. But she knew he'd be leaving in a few days. Who knew if he would come back?

Or if he would sell the farm?

The dark cloud of the unknown future hung over her. He'd seemed to embrace the farm life the last few days. How could he turn his back on all of this? How could he turn his back on her again?

"Penny for your thoughts," Jesse said next to her.

Rose threw a blossom into her bin, carried it to the UTV and switched it out for the last empty bin. "I was just thinking to myself it's nice to have you back." She omitted the part where she worried that he'd leave for good and sell the farm.

"It's been nice catching up with you and spending time together," he agreed, following her to a fresh row with dozens of blossoms waiting to be cut.

It was that time of day when dusk settled over the land, right before night fell. In the twilight, Rose could just make out Jesse's dark eyes. It made her heart ache just a little. The man had no idea the turmoil he could put her through with just one look.

"I know you're still deciding whether to keep the farm

or not," she heard herself say. "Regardless of what you choose, do you think we can stay in touch this time?"

Jesse sighed heavily. "I would love nothing more. But I think if I sell the farm, I'll probably be the last person you want to talk to."

She gave him a crooked smile. "You have a point. So, I guess you can't sell the farm."

Though Jesse laughed, she could tell she'd touched a nerve when he said, "I wish it were that easy."

Chapter Nine

On Friday morning, the first day of the Sunflower Festival, the farm came alive with activity. A stream of vendors and at least fifty volunteers arrived at the farm first thing. The festival was always a little crazy on the first day, but the rest of the weekend, it usually ran smoothly.

An hour before the noon opening, Rose gathered everyone around the barnyard to go over the schedule of events and answer any questions. Afterward, she noticed Jesse casually leaning against the barn door, watching her with an amused smirk on his face. He was devastatingly handsome in his navy blue firefighter uniform. She knew he was volunteering today but hadn't thought twice about what he would wear.

"Hey there. You clean up nice," she said, walking up to him. She wanted to ask if all firefighters looked half as good in their uniforms as him.

"Thanks. I figured I better look the part."

"You definitely do. So, what's up? Were you waiting on me?" Rose wore her yellow Sunflower Farms T-shirt like the rest of the staff, distinguishing them from the festival volunteers. She held a clipboard with the schedule in one hand, the other on her hip.

"Yeah. We have the fire truck in the field. I think it's where you wanted it. I was hoping you'd run out there and check it's in the right place before we pull everything out."

"I actually was heading that way. Come on, we'll walk out together."

On the way to the fire truck, they were stopped several times by volunteers, mostly old friends from church and high school who recognized Jesse. Many handshakes and hugs later, Rose and Jesse finally reached the fire truck.

His gaze roamed the area. "I see you put us next to the lineup of food trucks. I hope the festival visitors see us, too."

"It's strategy. People will wander by as they're checking out the food. Trust me, you'll get lots of foot traffic today."

"That makes sense. I can't believe how many people I've already run into today."

"I bet you'll see lots more before the day is over."

"I forgot how friendly everyone is here."

"Eagletin is a good place to live and to raise a family."

"I'm starting to see that."

Rose hoped he appreciated it enough not to sell it, but decided against mentioning it at that moment. He had to figure it out on his own. And if he didn't, she'd somehow deal with the loss—and her broken heart.

Just then, they were joined by another firefighter, also in a navy blue uniform. Jesse introduced them. "Rose, I would like you to meet my good buddy, Mike. Mike, meet Rose."

She shook his hand. "Thank you so much for volunteering today. I can't tell you how much we appreciate you donating your time."

"I am happy to be here for a good cause," Mike said with a wink. "If there's anything I can do for you, just let me know." He held Rose's hand a little longer than necessary.

Jesse gave his friend a dirty look, and inwardly Rose smiled, wondering if Jesse was a little jealous. When was the last time she had two men interested in her romantically?

"I'm sure Rose is busy and needs to get going," Jesse said to Mike, who at last let go of her hand.

"I won't keep you then, but I hope you'll stop by later," Mike said to her.

"Definitely," Rose answered. She gave Jesse a big grin as she walked away. It wouldn't hurt Jesse to think there was a little competition, and if she were being honest with herself, it was nice being noticed for once.

By the afternoon, the temperature crept up to the eighties. The crowd was thick, and visitors kept coming. Other than a few hiccups, the festival had got off to a good start. Grammy stopped by to chat with Rose at the festival information booth.

"There you are," Grammy said. A tall older gentleman, with gray hair and glasses, was at her side.

"Grammy! I was wondering when I'd see you," Rose said as she set down her clipboard. Her eyes went to Grammy's guest.

"Let me introduce you to my new friend Bob,"

Grammy said. "Bob, this is my beautiful granddaughter, Rose."

Rose shook Bob's hand, laughing. "I don't know about beautiful. More like sweaty and exhausted. But it's nice to meet you."

"You're beautiful all the same. The outdoors and sunshine give you a healthy glow," Bob said.

Rose already liked the man. "Thank you. Welcome to our farm. Are you two having fun at the festival?"

"It's been nice catching up with folks," Grammy said. "I ran into Jesse by the fire truck. I'm surprised he's still here."

"Grammy, please give it a rest. Jesse promised to help with the festival, and the firefighters have been a big hit."

She raised her brows. "Yeah, a hit with all the single ladies," she said with a chuckle.

Rose rolled her eyes, then felt her phone buzz in her pocket. She pulled out the phone and answered, "Hello?"

"Rose, it's Lolly. The guy running the kissing booth had to leave early. Do you have someone else who can work it?"

"I'll figure something out. Don't worry, I'll take care of it." Rose hung up and blew out an exasperated breath. The kissing booth was a big moneymaker, and she hated to lose out on what it could make in the next four hours. Yeah, the booth was a little silly, maybe cheesy, and definitely old-fashioned, but it had become part of the fun that folks expected.

She suddenly had a brilliant idea. She knew a certain handsome fireman who didn't have a shy bone in his body.

Rose said goodbye to Grammy and Bob, then headed for the fire truck. When she approached, Mike had a crowd of little kids sitting in the grass listening to him talk about fighting fires like it was career day at school. The kids were mesmerized.

Jesse stood off to the side, leaning against the truck.

Rose sidled up next to him. "Hey there. Mike is so good with them."

"Tell me about it. I think he missed his calling." Jesse pushed away from the truck and straightened. "How are things going?"

"Good. But…" Rose gave him a sheepish look. "I have a favor to ask."

"Sure, anything," Jesse said.

"I need someone to take over the kissing booth."

His face fell. "Anything but that."

"Why not? Please. I'll owe you."

"Why don't you do it?" he asked.

"Because I'm running the festival. I can't be tied down to one booth."

He shifted his weight from one foot to the other. "Is there any chance you'll take no for an answer?"

"Nope," Rose said.

"Fine. Show me what you want me to do."

They left the fire truck in Mike's capable hands, and Rose led Jesse to the kissing booth.

Jesse hesitated in the front of it and read the sign they had added. "Sunflower Farms Sweetheart… Oh man. You're kidding, right?"

"Come on. You can do it. Jump on back there." Gently, Rose pushed him along.

He stepped inside the booth. "What do I have to do?"

Rose pointed to a second smaller sign and read it off, "Five dollars a kiss from the Sunflower Farms Sweetheart. All proceeds go to the Taylor Family Fire Fund."

Jesse crossed his arms over his chest, "I don't know about this. And I don't know how I feel about kissing strangers."

Rose really couldn't blame him for balking. "Relax. It's for a good cause. You're a nice-looking guy. People will pay you five dollars a kiss."

He narrowed his eyes at her. "What kind of kiss are we talking about?"

She laughed. "Don't worry. I promise nothing more than a kiss on the cheek."

Resigned, Jesse agreed. "Fine. I guess I can do that. But don't tell Mike or the rest of the guys where I went, or I'll never hear the end of it."

"Agreed. Hey, look, you have your first customer."

Mrs. Dawkins handed a five-dollar bill to Rose, who put it in the cashbox. Jesse leaned down and planted a quick peck on her cheek.

"Thank you, Jesse." She giggled and made a big deal out of the kiss, all in good fun.

Jesse laughed along, until he spotted more ladies coming over. Rose's grandmother was next in line, with Bob good-naturedly waiting with her.

"You're still here?" Grammy asked Jesse.

"Yes, ma'am, but at the moment, I wish I were anywhere but here," Jesse answered in good humor.

"Grammy, you're not allowed to tease him," Rose said. "He's doing me a favor by working the booth."

"Honey, he's doing us all a favor. I do love a man in uniform." Grammy held up a five-dollar bill and waited for her kiss.

Jesse squeezed his eyes shut and mumbled, "What have I gotten myself into?"

Rose patted him on the arm. "I have a feeling you're going to be very popular." She walked away, chuckling as she saw the line getting longer and longer...

The next day of the festival, Saturday, was just as busy. Jesse purposefully stayed clear of the kissing booth. He made a mental note never to let Rose talk him into doing that again. The afternoon had been awkward and uncomfortable, but he'd managed it okay. Though, he had to admit, she'd been right. He'd raised a lot of money for the Taylors, and he'd only had to sacrifice his pride to do it.

Mike brought the fire engine back out, and he and Jesse stood under the warm October sunshine and greeted folks as they wandered by. Kids were in awe of the truck and enjoyed climbing on it, then took turns trying on the gear. Elementary school boys and girls stared up at them with a bit of hero worship, like they were as great as superheroes.

Jesse remembered being the same way when he was a kid. He also noticed some of the moms staring a little too much as they waited for their kids. Mike enjoyed the attention and flirted shamelessly while Jesse kept everything professional.

Like yesterday, Mike gave talks whenever a crowd gathered. Jesse leaned on the truck and listened as Mike recounted a tale of the worst fire he'd ever seen and how he saved the day. Yeah, Mike liked to embellish some, but it was a good story.

An older couple stopped next to Jesse. "Is that you, Jesse Cooper?" the woman asked.

Jesse recognized the man and woman instantly. They were Rose's parents. They were a little bit grayer and older than he remembered, but it was definitely them. He'd know their warm smiles anywhere. "Anne, John, it's good to see you. How are you?"

Rose's mom pulled Jesse into a big hug, and he leaned down to embrace the petite woman. When he straightened, John greeted him with a pat on the shoulder, saying, "We're good! Rose told us you were here. She said to follow the trail to the fire truck, and we'd find you. Although she never said anything about the crowd."

Jesse chuckled. "The crowd isn't for me. It's for the master entertainer over there." He pointed toward Mike. "Stick around long enough, and you can hear how he single-handedly saved the world from the largest fire ever…or something like that."

"As interesting as that sounds, we actually want to hear about you. How are you? We were surprised to hear you were back in Eagletin," John said.

Jesse inhaled deeply as he tried to think of how to put it into words. How was he? Confused. Unsure what to do with the farm. Unsure about what was happening between him and their daughter.

Instead of saying all that, he said what they wanted to hear. "I'm doing great. As you can see—" he gestured toward his uniform "—I'm a firefighter, and it's a great career. I've also been out here at the farm all week, cleaning out my folks' home. Thought I would stay to help with the festival."

"Does this mean you plan to be at the farm more often?" Anne asked. She stared up at him with the same intelligent blue eyes as her daughter. She reminded him of Rose in every way: small stature, big personality.

Jesse shrugged. "I haven't decided. As you know, there's a lot of history for me here, some good and some bad. I'm not sure how involved I want to be."

"That's understandable, though I'm sure Rose loves having you back," Anne said.

John interjected, "Whatever you decide, the farm will be in good hands with Rose."

"I agree," Jesse said at once. "Rose is amazing, and what she's done with this place is something else." He would hazard a guess she hadn't had a chance to tell them that he might sell the property. But he wasn't going to bring it up now.

"Yeah, this whole sunflower business brought the farm back from the brink of bankruptcy. It was all her idea to open it up to the public," John said.

It only made Jesse admire Rose even more. "It was a great idea. Who knew this would go over so well?"

"So, are you married now?" Anne asked, just as blunt as her daughter. John subtly elbowed her.

Jesse tried to hold in a chuckle. "No, ma'am. I'm not married and currently not dating anyone." He knew what was coming before she could even get it out.

"You know, our Rosie is still single," Anne said.

"Oh? You don't say." Jesse played along.

John laid an arm over his wife's shoulder to usher her away. "Come on, Anne. Let Jesse be. He's been back five minutes, and you're already playing matchmaker. Let's go find something to eat. We can catch up later." He waved goodbye as they walked on.

Jesse waved back, relieved that John had intervened. He'd always liked her parents. If only he could have had the same kind of happy childhood she'd had.

The day flew by until it was nearly time for the barn dance that evening. As the sun set, Jesse went back to the house to clean up and change out of his uniform into jeans and a long-sleeved Western-style shirt appropriate for the theme. By the time he stepped back outside, night had fallen.

Under a half-moon, the thousands of white lights they'd hung lit the barnyard. Couples danced underneath them while other folks hung out on the perimeter socializing. Jesse made his way through the throngs of people, stopping repeatedly to greet old friends as he passed by. It made him miss small-town life like he never had before. This would be what he gave up if he sold the farm.

He'd have to give up Rose, too, because she would never forgive him.

The countdown had begun. Jesse had one more full day to spend at the farm, then he would return to work in Jacksonville. And he'd have to get back to the investor with a decision on whether to sell. A week ago, Jesse had made up his mind that he wanted nothing to do with the farm. He hadn't counted on the good memories that flooded back or hearing the stories of how his dad had changed.

He also hadn't planned on how much he still felt for Rose. It was hard to make a clearheaded decision with her around, when all he wanted to do was please her. Perhaps it was for the best he was leaving. But that didn't mean he couldn't enjoy tonight.

Jesse searched for Rose in the crowd. When he found her, she was on the dance floor in another man's arms, moving to a slow song. She wore a red dress and cowboy boots, her honey-brown hair falling over her shoulders in glossy waves. She was beautiful, and Jesse couldn't take his eyes off her.

A hint of jealousy sprang up that it wasn't him holding her. He tamped down the feeling. She wasn't his girlfriend, and even if she was, she could dance with whomever she wanted.

The song came to an end, and the guy let go of Rose. Springing into action, Jesse weaved through the crowded dance floor to get to her before someone else snatched her up. A couple people recognized him as he worked his way through. Jesse nodded in acknowledgment but kept on his pursuit.

Rose saw him headed her way, and from across the dance floor, their eyes locked. A wide smile spread across her face.

Jesse liked it when she was happy. He liked it too much.

Finally he reached her and held his hand out in invitation. "May I have this dance?" he asked as the next song started.

"Yes," she said, placing her hand in his.

Jesse pulled her into his arms. It felt like home.

They swayed in time to the music. The two of them together like this was like a dream. He'd be content to stay this way forever.

Rose tilted her head up. "I barely saw you today. How did things go?" she asked.

"Great, especially since I wasn't stuck in the kissing booth again," he said with a grin.

Rose laughed. "You survived, as I knew you would."

"With no help from you. You dropped me off and left me to fend off the wolves."

"I wouldn't call little old ladies wolves."

"Ha, that's what you think."

Her eyes sparkled under the lights. "It was the uniform. Women love to see a guy in uniform."

"Are you saying you like me in uniform?"

"Maybe," she conceded. "Now shut up and dance with me." Her arms tightened around him, and she laid her head against his chest.

Inwardly Jesse smiled. Why did it make him happy to know that Rose liked him in his firefighter uniform? All he knew was that he didn't care one bit about all those single moms at the kissing booth. It was Rose he longed to impress.

Rose held on to Jesse as they floated around the dance floor. With her arms wrapped around him, she leaned into his warmth. Her cheek rested against his chest, and she inhaled his fresh clean scent. Content, she sighed.

She was happy. She had thoroughly enjoyed spending the week with him, but he would leave soon. She had to be prepared, but deep down, she knew it would still hurt.

Jesse interrupted her thoughts. "You look pretty tonight, Rose. But then again, you always look pretty."

Her face flushed at his praise, and she was thankful for the low lighting. "Thank you. You look nice, too."

Jesse laughed. "You're just saying that because you have to be nice back."

"Yeah, you're right," she teased, and they both laughed.

"So, what do you think of the dance?" she asked.

"I'm impressed by how many people came out for it and what a success it is. And the string lights look spectacular. Whoever helped you with them should be given an award."

Rose rolled her eyes. "Give me a break, if I'd left it up to you, they'd all be crooked."

Jesse laughed.

Rose added, "Seriously, now you can see why I've been running around all week like a chicken with its head cut off. But it was worth it. We're going to raise a lot of money this weekend for the Taylors."

"I forgot to tell you, Mike and I have been collecting money from the guys at the firehouse. We've raised $3,500 to add to the fund."

Rose gasped. "Wow! That's wonderful. Make sure you tell the guys how much we appreciate their help."

"I will, but they were happy to chip in. A lot of them were there the night the Taylors' house burned down. It was heartbreaking."

She shook her head. "I can only imagine."

Jesse and Rose moved in sync across the dance floor. She'd forgotten what a good dancer he was, so light on his feet. And he knew how to lead. She'd be content to dance with him the rest of the night, but too soon the song came to an end. She reluctantly stepped out of his arms, though he didn't seem to want it to be over, either.

A popular line dance started, and the floor quickly became packed. Jesse grabbed Rose's hand and led her through the crowd to the refreshment stand. He released her hand once they were in the clear. Rose was disappointed he let go.

"Would you like a drink?" he asked, smiling at her.

Rose felt her stomach do a little flip-flop. She tucked her hair behind one ear. "I'd love to try the hot apple cider. It's Lolly's recipe."

Turning to the lady serving drinks, he ordered two. Together they took their steaming cups and walked away from the crowd and loud music. Rose took a careful sip. The combination of cinnamon and apple was delicious.

"Let's find somewhere to sit," she suggested. "My feet are killing me. If I've learned anything today, these boots are not for dancing."

Jesse laughed. "I guess they aren't the boots you use to muck the stalls."

"They are not."

They left the dance behind and strolled into the darkness beyond the barnyard. With the music fading and all the visitors forgotten, they reached the empty picnic tables and sat down next to each other under the moonlight.

Rose let out a big sigh and pulled one boot off, then the other. She closed her eyes and savored being side by side with Jesse. "I have a new appreciation for what you do," Jesse said into the silence.

Rose opened her eyes and sat up a little straighter. "Why do you say that?"

"I've watched you manage this farm all week, juggle the many problems that come with it, work from dawn to dusk, and still, you manage to give yourself wholly to this festival all for the purpose of raising money for the Taylor family. And you do it with a smile on your face..." Jesse hesitated, then leaned to the side and gently bumped shoulders with her, adding, "I mean, most of the time you have a smile on your face," he teased.

"Most of the time," she agreed. "I think you know by now, this farm is my life. It comes from my heart."

"I can see that."

The moon lit the area enough that in the distance Rose could see the sunflower fields. Soon the flowers would die for the winter, and they would have to start the cycle all over again and plant a new crop in the spring. Would Jesse be around to help?

A slow song started in the distance. The light melody carried across the fields.

"Come on. You owe me another dance," Jesse said.

"Please don't make me walk back." Rose slipped her boots back on as she said it.

Jesse pulled her up, and they stood facing one another. "Dance with me here, then," he suggested with a serious expression.

The romance of it all wasn't lost on Rose…a dance in the moonlight with her old love. Never in a million years had she imagined he'd come back home or that they would reunite. And here they were. Together again. But for how long?

She looped her arms around his neck and stared into his eyes. They slowly danced to the distant music, both quiet as they studied one another. She would forever remember the way he looked under the moonlight, and how she imagined there was love in his eyes when he looked at her, whether it was true or not.

When the song ended, Jesse leaned down and kissed her, soft and sweet.

She had worked so hard to keep her emotions for him in check all this time. But she was worn out from it and just wanted to love him. Even if only for a few days.

Jesse ended the kiss. Then like a gentleman, he walked her back to the dance.

What did this mean for them? For her? For the farm? Rose had more questions than answers.

Chapter Ten

Jesse turned into the church parking lot early Sunday morning and shut off the engine. The lot was already almost full, which was impressive. Half the church members had been at the barn dance until late last night.

"Glad to see the festival didn't hurt turnout this morning," Rose said as she glanced around the parking lot. Dressed in a simple yellow sundress, she somehow looked fresh and rested after the busy weekend.

"I was thinking the same thing," Jesse said. "It would have been too easy to sleep in today."

"Nah, the festival's not over. Sunday church is just a much-needed break in the middle. Also, the Taylors will be at the service, and the pastor will be bringing them onstage to talk about the festival. Anybody who hasn't come out yet will be gently reminded to show their support."

Jesse laughed. "You mean guilted into coming to the festival."

Rose laughed. "Your words, not mine."

Inside the church, Jesse was stopped over and over, shaking hands with old friends and being introduced to new ones. Once they were settled in the pew, he glanced over at Rose, and she grinned back.

"What are you smiling about?" he asked.

She shrugged, then admitted, "I just like having you here with me. It's nice."

He reached over and squeezed her hand affectionately. "Yeah, it is."

Just before the service started, Lolly slipped in next to Rose. They exchanged a few words and giggled a little before Lolly said hi to Jesse.

A minute later, Rose's parents and her grandmother walked down the aisle and filed into the empty seats on the other side of Lolly. Anne set her purse on the floor, leaned over and gave quick hugs to Rose, Lolly and Jesse. "I've missed you all so much," she said as she sat down.

"Good morning," Rose's dad greeted everyone as her grandmother waved at them.

The service began, and Jesse sat up in his seat, a little nervous. It had been so long since he'd attended church.

Pastor Ronnie's sermon was on forgiveness, and it felt like everything he said had been meant for Jesse. He'd come to church to please Rose, but never once had he considered how it might affect him. Like everything else lately, he'd misjudged it. In the end, the service gave him more to think about when it came to his dad and the forgiveness Jesse withheld.

The hour passed by quickly, and soon Jesse was dropping Rose off at her apartment.

"Thanks for driving," she said as she slid out of the car. "I'm heading up to change and eat lunch real quick before the festival starts. You want to come up for a sandwich?"

"Thanks, but no. I feel like driving around a little before this place gets busy again."

Rose narrowed her eyes at him. "Are you okay? You've been awfully quiet."

Jesse smiled reassuringly. "I'm fine. I just need a few minutes alone."

"Okay, but you know where to find me if you want to talk or if you change your mind about the sandwich."

Jesse nodded back. With a heavy heart, he drove over to the sunflower fields. He parked on the edge where he and Rose had picked flowers. Some folks had a view of the mountains or a beach, but how many had a breath-taking view of a majestic sunflower field? He took his time and appreciated the sea of yellow and green underneath the vast blue sky.

This was all his.

And this had been his father's. The same man who had shunned Jesse and made life unbearable after his mother died.

He got out of the car and strolled down a row. The sunflowers were as tall as him, and it felt like he walked through a floral tunnel that had no end in sight. He shoved his hands in his pockets as he kicked up the ground in front of him. His pace was leisurely while his mind wandered.

Who was he kidding? He wasn't punishing his father by staying mad at him. The man was dead. He was only hurting himself.

Maybe it was time he saw everything from his dad's point of view. The man had been crushed when his be-loved wife died, and it was that unbearable pain that caused him to treat Jesse so poorly. His dad hadn't acted that way because he didn't love Jesse. He acted that way because he'd lost his true love and he couldn't cope with it.

Those three years after her death, he had loved Jesse. He'd just been too torn up to show it properly. His actions were overshadowed by tragic loss.

Did that make it okay the way his old man acted? No. But now Jesse could see it through the eyes of an adult. And along with that realization, he also knew it was time to forgive him.

Apparently, his dad's outlook on life changed when he found God. He must have finally accepted the loss of his wife and he must have regretted the way he'd treated Jesse. In the end, he became a better person.

Jesse sadly wished he had been around for that. He wished he'd called him back when his dad left that message. He wished he'd been there for him when he was sick. He wished he had returned in time for that…but he knew that wishing would get him nowhere.

What he could do was forgive him and finally let it all go—his father's failures and his own.

And that was exactly what he did.

In the middle of the sunflower field, Jesse closed his eyes, lifted his head toward the sky and sucked in a breath. As he let out the air, peace settled over him.

Jesse forgave his father, and he forgave himself.

Turnout on the last day of the Sunflower Festival was great, but Rose was happy to see the huge event come to an end. The remaining volunteers finished cleanup just before sunset. With the busy afternoon, Rose hadn't had a chance to speak to Jesse again.

The lights were on in the main house, so she headed over. Like a moth to the flame, she was drawn to him, carrying two glasses of iced tea to share.

Jesse answered the door. "Hey there," he said, sounding genuinely happy to see her.

"Hi… I brought refreshments. I thought we could sit down and celebrate the success of the festival." Rose lifted one glass and offered it to him.

Jesse took it and opened the door all the way. "Thanks. Come on in."

"I thought we could sit on the porch, like the old days."

He looked surprised. "Oh…sounds good."

They walked over to the old-fashioned porch swing and sat down. It creaked as they pushed off. Rose made a face. "I hope this thing doesn't break. I guess it's pretty old."

Jesse shrugged. "Nah, it's fine. I gave it a test drive the other day."

Rose lifted her glass, "I'd like to make a toast. Here's to another successful year of the Sunflower Festival and to your first festival ever."

"To the Sunflower Festival," Jesse repeated, then clinked her glass with his.

Rose sipped her tea, then set her glass on the floor. "We raised over $43,000," she announced, "and it's all going to the Taylors."

Jesse seemed astonished by the amount. "Wow. I

never dreamed you'd raise that much. That's something else."

Rose grinned at him. "I know. It was so much work but well worth it."

"I had no idea the farm could make that much money."

"Keep in mind it was a charity event, so we charged more than normal for admission. Plus, we had a couple thousand people attending this weekend. That's a lot of people paying admission. We don't make as much on our normal weekends, or have that many visitors, but we still do pretty well."

"That's unbelievable. My turn now," Jesse said as he raised his glass. "Here's to you, Rose. You are the backbone to this place. You are an incredible woman."

"Thank you," she said, touched by his words. They clinked glasses again, then sipped their tea as the swing rocked back and forth.

"Did you catch Pastor Ronnie in the dunking booth? I heard it took a while before someone finally dunked him," Rose said.

"Yeah, I did," he said innocently. "Who do you think nailed him?"

"Was it you?" Rose laughed out loud. "I wish I'd seen that."

Jesse chuckled. "I'm pretty sure some kids recorded it on their phones."

"I'll have to get my hands on that footage. I'll bet Pastor Ronnie wasn't too happy, especially after he welcomed you back with open arms."

"Trust me, there's no hard feelings," Jesse said.

"Like you're one to talk about hard feelings. You're still angry at your dad."

He didn't make the quick comeback she was expecting. He shifted uncomfortably next to her and cleared his throat.

Rose could kick herself. "I'm sorry. I shouldn't have said that. That was insensitive."

"It's okay. Actually, I had a breakthrough today. I've been wrestling with this all week. Today I finally made peace with my dad. I forgave him."

It was Rose's turn to be shocked. "Really?"

"Yeah, really," Jesse said lightly. He leaned back and rested an arm over the back of the swing.

Her heart melted just a little. "I'm proud of you. I know it wasn't easy, but it was the right thing to do."

"It was. With what you said about him changing and then finding the newspaper clippings and add in the pastor's sermon this morning… I knew it was time to let the past go. I feel like a burden's been lifted. I didn't realize how unhealthy it was, carrying around all that baggage. All that pain and hate, eating away at me for so many years. I also finally have a clearer picture of why he acted that way. I think it really comes down to how much he loved my mom and the fact he couldn't deal with her loss. He still loved me, he just couldn't show it because of the pain he was in."

"I think you're right. I wish you could have been around after he found God. He was a different man."

"I wish I had, too. I'm also sorry I wasn't here for him when he was sick."

"It's okay. He was in good hands, and we gave him lots of love until the end."

"Thank you for that."

"You're welcome. Now, maybe you can put all this to rest and finally be happy."

Jesse looked thoughtful as he stared out into the yard. The sun had disappeared over the horizon, and they swung quietly in the glow of the porch light. The night air was chilly, and Rose wrapped her arms across her chest for warmth. A comfortable silence stretched between them.

"Are you really leaving tomorrow?" she asked at last.

Jesse looked at her, then rested his outstretched arm on her shoulder. He pulled her into his side and ran a hand down her chilled arm. "Yeah, I am," he said with a touch of resignation.

"Are you coming back?"

"I don't know."

"You don't know?" Rose asked. "I thought for sure if you forgave your dad, you would want to keep the farm."

"That's just it, I don't know. I need to go back home and do some soul-searching. You have to understand, the farm was never my dream."

"I know," Rose said quietly. "It was mine."

Rose finished up her tea, made her excuses, and left. She'd wanted to celebrate their successful weekend together, but their conversation only put a damper on everything.

Rose didn't understand Jesse. He acted like he enjoyed her company, yet he planned to leave and not come back. What about her? Why wouldn't he come back for her?

She should have listened to her own instincts and protected her heart. Now it was too late.

He would break her heart all over again.

Chapter Eleven

Just like he said he would, early Monday morning, Jesse gave Rose a quick hug goodbye, then left. There were no promises made or any assurances about their relationship. Just a simple goodbye. Rose shouldn't be disappointed. She'd known all along this was coming. Yet here she was, upset and frustrated all the same.

Church volunteers helped take down the festival decorations and return the games and booths. Then life went on like before the festival, and more important, before Jesse's appearance.

Regardless of what happened or didn't happen with Rose's love life, she had a farm to run. She buried herself in work in an attempt to keep herself busy and her mind off Jesse. He'd been gone a few days…but who was counting?

She led Missy and Moe to a pasture to graze, then went to the barn to milk Betsy. She grabbed a pail and stool and sat next to the cow. She patted her side, and Betsy flicked her tail and mooed in greeting. Rose efficiently milked her, all the while her mind on Jesse.

Those old feelings for Jesse had definitely come back. There was no denying she still loved him. And either he was the best actor that ever lived or he felt something for her, too. She tried to stay positive and believe he would return to the farm, but the longer she went without hearing from him, the more doubt filled her mind. What if she'd been wrong to trust him again? What if he left for another ten years?

She had to remind herself that she was a strong woman. She didn't need a man in her life to be fulfilled.

When Rose walked Betsy out to join the horses in the pasture, she heard the irrigation system turn on in the sunflower field. A cloud of mist surrounded the blooms, raining down much needed moisture. Another reminder of how much it meant to have Jesse's help last week. He'd saved the day when it came to the drought.

Rose felt her phone buzz in her pocket. She pulled it out, unable to suppress the hope that it was finally him. *Come on, Rose*, she silently reprimanded herself.

The text was from her mom. Do you want to come over for dinner tonight?

No, she wanted to have dinner with Jesse.

It was aggravating how disappointed Rose was that it wasn't him.

Jesse or no Jesse, Rose had to eat. She fired back a quick text. Sure, what time?

How about six? I can't wait to see you.

Sounds good!

Her mom sent back a kissy-face emoji with some hearts.

Rose smiled, shoved her phone back in her pocket and headed toward her apartment. A nice black sedan coming down the long driveway caught her eye. It rolled to a stop in front of the gift shop.

Tony saw the car, too, as he was walking back from the sunflower fields. Rose waved him off, letting him know that she would take care of it. When she approached the car, a man in a business suit rolled down his window.

"I'm sorry, we're closed today," Rose said.

"I was actually looking for Jesse Cooper," he said, looking up at her through dark sunglasses.

"He's not here, he lives in Jacksonville. Is there something I can help you with?"

"Would you mind if I drove around the farm? I'm the investor buying this place."

Her stomach lurched, and suddenly she felt like she would throw up. Coolly, she said, "Now's not a good time. Please call to make an appointment." Abruptly, she stormed off before the man could say anything else.

She flew upstairs to her apartment, fumbling with the door. Her shaky hands would not cooperate, but finally she got the door open, stepped in and slammed it shut.

"Stupid, stupid, stupid," she said angrily in the silence of the room. She paced around the studio furiously. She didn't know whether to scream or cry.

So that was why Jesse hadn't called her. He'd decided to sell the farm and couldn't face her. Coward.

She'd been a fool to fall for him again. The man had destroyed her once. What had she expected this time? She should never have let her guard down and trusted him.

Rose did a couple more laps around the apartment.

Finally she came to a halt, pulled out her phone and called Jesse. It rang several times, but there was no answer.

She hung up when the voice mail came on. She needed to speak with him. She needed to know how he could do this to her. If he wasn't answering her calls, then she would go down to the firehouse to talk to him.

Grabbing her purse, she ran downstairs. As she was getting in the car, she had an idea. She would need to stop at her parents' house on the way.

Jesse sat on his bunk, exhausted. It was the first time he'd had a chance to rest in days. They'd been fighting an uncontained forest fire, another result of the nasty drought. He'd taken a couple of extra shifts to help out—and to keep his mind off Rose. The problem was, he still hadn't decided what to do about the farm.

One of his coworkers called out, "Cooper, you have a visitor."

"Okay. Coming." Jesse sighed, then got up to see who his visitor was. He wasn't expecting anyone.

In the firehouse lobby, he found Rose peering out the window, her back to him. His heart filled with warmth. Exhausted or not, he was glad to see her. "Rose. I can't believe these guys left you standing out here and didn't invite you inside."

She turned. Immediately, Jesse knew she was mad. Her mouth was set in a hard line, and her eyes shot daggers at him. She balled her hands next to her sides and stood ramrod straight.

His smile dropped. "I'm happy to see you but what's wrong?"

"Don't try to be charming with me, it's not going to work. Why didn't you tell me first?" Her words were loud and angry, and some of the guys came to the doorway to see what was going on.

Jesse shooed them away and shut the door for privacy. He turned back to Rose and said calmly, "Come on, let's take a walk outside." He took a step toward her and she shrugged him off. He had never seen her so angry.

"I don't want to take a walk," she barked.

"Okay, fine, we don't have to walk. But I don't know why you're mad."

"Really? You can't figure it out? Let me say it then… I know you went through with the deal to sell the farm," she snapped.

"What?" Jesse felt like he was in an alternate universe. What was happening? "I don't know what you're talking about."

"Don't play dumb. The buyer came out to the farm to look around. How could you do that? You should have warned me."

Jesse shook his head, "Again, I don't know what you're talking about. I haven't made any deal. I haven't even made a decision on whether to keep it or not, for that matter."

He could tell Rose wasn't listening. She was too fired up to talk rationally. She paced back and forth in the small lobby. She was dressed in T-shirt, jeans and work boots like she'd come straight from the farm. Her hair was pulled back into her usual ponytail.

When she started talking again, it was more to herself. "I knew you were going to be trouble when you came back. But did I listen to my instincts? No, I played right into your hands, like I was some teenager with a crush... Waiting for you to call me, waiting for your texts, like I didn't have a lick of sense." She was agitated, clearly not her normal self.

Abruptly, she came to a halt. "Let me buy the farm. My parents said they would help me with the money. Together, we can buy you out. Please don't sell it to a stranger."

Jesse rubbed his jaw. This was not what he'd expected. "I don't know what's going on, but you're misinformed."

That only made her angrier. "You're right, I was misinformed the minute I started trusting you again."

He held up his hands. "Can I interrupt for a minute?"

She grew silent and crossed her arms defensively as she waited for him to finish.

"I haven't sold anything. I've been so busy in the last few days with the forest fire along I-95 that I've barely had time to eat or sleep, much less sell my family farm. But trust me, you will be the first person I inform if I decide to sell. I promise I'll give you the first chance to bid on it, if that's what you want. I won't do anything behind your back."

Rose stared at him blankly. He could see the wheels turning in her head, but she was still spitting mad.

"Well, I would hope so," she said curtly, then pivoted and left in a huff.

What just happened? Jesse's heart raced from the encounter, but he felt like he'd handled it as well as he could have.

Mike cracked the door open and leaned in. "I couldn't help but notice Rose was here. She didn't look so happy with you. What's going on? Are you okay, man?"

Jesse blew out a big breath. "That woman is going to be the end of me."

Mike laughed. "Aren't they all?"

"She thought I sold the farm." Jesse ran a hand through his hair as he followed Mike back toward the firehouse kitchen.

"Well, are you going to sell it?"

"I haven't decided." Jesse grabbed a cold bottle of water out of the refrigerator and took a swig.

"What's been stopping you from deciding?"

"Originally, I didn't want the farm because it reminded me too much of my dad and what I went through with him. But I finally made my peace with that. Now it's more about what kind of career I want. I can't decide if I want to be a firefighter or a farmer. I've built a life here, I've got a good career, but I'm not sure I want to do this for the rest of my life. Meanwhile, being back on the farm last week felt good. It felt right, living the country life and being home again. The biggest surprise of all was reconnecting with Rose. She's an amazing person."

Mike shrugged. "I don't understand what the problem

is. Why can't you own the farm *and* be a firefighter? Do both."

Jesse stared at him. Now that he'd forgiven his father, there really wasn't anything holding him back. Why hadn't he realized that? And there was a reason Rose was a distraction. Because he had genuine feelings for her. But did she feel the same way? She'd repeatedly told him she loved the farm, but did she love him, too?

After Rose left the firehouse, she drove back to the farm still fuming mad, but also embarrassed by her rash behavior.

If Jesse had ever thought about getting back together with her, surely she'd just blown it. She had assumed the worst, gone to the firehouse ready to tear into him, and he'd been the levelheaded one. Not her.

Slowly, her mind cleared. This whole thing was a wakeup call to the very real possibility that he could still sell the farm. Just because he spent one week with her and she'd imagined the old feelings between them were still strong, it didn't mean he felt the same way. He had a whole other life now. Maybe he didn't want to give it all up for an old girlfriend. Maybe he was happy with the way things were.

The one positive thing that came out of this fiasco was that he promised he would give her the first crack at buying the farm, and that was a relief. Though that would mean he wasn't returning, and deep down inside that hurt.

At six, Rose arrived at her parents' house for dinner. By then, she was over the anger and completely regretting her behavior. She gave a quick knock at the door, then walked in.

Her dad was in the recliner in the living room watching the news. "Rose, come in," he said when he saw her. He stood up and wrapped her in a warm hug. "How's my girl?"

"I'm okay." *Not good.*

Her mom and grandmother came out from the kitchen to greet her with a hug apiece.

"You're right on time, and everything's ready if you want to eat," her mom said.

The four of them went to the kitchen where the table was already set. Her mom set down a roast next to some side dishes. The aroma wafted over to Rose, but it did nothing for her. She had been so upset all day that she barely had an appetite. She fixed a plate anyway. Her mom had gone to a lot of trouble making a nice meal, and she didn't want to be rude.

Rose had barely swallowed her first bite when her mom asked, "How did it go with Jesse? Is he going to let you buy the farm?"

Grammy's brow lifted questioningly.

"Jesse may sell the farm," Rose explained to her, "so Mom and Dad have agreed to help me buy it."

"That sounds like a wonderful idea. You've done so much for that place, you should be the one to buy it," Grammy said.

"I know. Anyway, I went up to the firehouse where he works and asked if he would give us the first chance to make a bid for the house, and he agreed he would."

Suddenly Rose crumbled. She put her head in her hand and closed her eyes.

Rose's mom rubbed her shoulder comfortingly. "Honey, what's wrong? That's good news, isn't it?"

Rose dropped her hand from her face and took a ragged breath. "It is good news, I just hate the way I behaved. I was so upset that I went in there yelling at him like some lunatic. I made such a scene. I should never have done that. I could just die of embarrassment."

Rose's mom smiled with understanding. "It's not the end of the world. I'm sure if you apologized, he would accept it."

"I know. You're right."

They talked more about the farm, and Rose realized her parents were genuinely excited about going into a partnership with her to own the farm. Grammy even said she'd pitch in and give Rose an early inheritance gift if she needed more financial help.

She really had the most supportive family ever.

Somehow Rose made it through dinner, but she didn't hang around like she usually would. Instead, she wanted to go back to the farm, to be alone and lick her wounds.

When she turned down the driveway toward the farm, her headlights lit the familiar path. Her home. She parked next to the gift shop and got out.

Instead of going upstairs to her apartment, Rose walked over to the main house. Once again, it was empty and dark, like it had been for the past year before Jesse decided to show up. She sat down on the porch swing with a heavy sigh and looked up at the sky. The moon and stars peeked out between the clouds. It was so beautiful and peaceful out there. Why would anyone want to give this up?

Each creak and moan of the old swing reminded her of the night she and Jesse sat on the porch after the festival. She'd felt so close to him. Had it been an act? If it wasn't, she'd probably scared him away after today.

Regret and heartache filled her.

He'd broken her trust ten years ago when he left her, and it was still affecting her. She had believed the worst of him today instead of giving him a chance to explain. She should have trusted him.

Rose pulled out her phone for the umpteenth time and willed him to call. But she knew it wasn't happening tonight. Maybe never.

She tapped the screen and started a new text message.

I hope you will accept my sincere apology for barging into your work and being outright ugly to you. You didn't deserve that. You were right, I was misinformed. I am sorry I jumped to conclusions. I hope you will forgive me.

With her finger hovering above the screen, Rose hesitated a heartbeat. At last she gathered her courage and hit Send. She knew she should shove the phone back in her pocket and forget about it, but instead she sat there and pathetically stared at the text, hoping for a reply.

The message note went from Delivered to Read.

Three little dots danced up and down on the screen. Jesse was typing something on the other end.

Rose held her breath, hoping it was the same level-headed guy from before.

The reply came through: Who is this?

What? Rose sat up straighter.

The three dots started dancing again, then a new message popped up.

Just kidding. There's nothing to forgive. I've already forgotten about it. You should, too.

Rose smiled, then texted back.

Thank you...and you're not funny!

His simple reply was YW.

You're welcome.

Rose would take it.

She leaned back on the swing and gently pushed off again. In the distance, the wind picked up, and dry leaves skittered across the yard. Cool air moved in and sent a chill up her bare arms. Soon the patter of rain surrounded her, slow at first, and then crushing. Lightning streaked across the sky, followed by thunder seconds later.

Rose smiled to herself. The rain had finally come.

Sunday morning, Rose followed Lolly into church and found their usual seats on the third row. Soon after, her parents and grandmother joined them. In the few minutes before the service started, everyone was talking about the storm that hit earlier in the week and how much they'd needed the rain.

Rose set her purse on her lap, then leaned back in the pew. She glanced down at the empty seat next to her and couldn't help but think of Jesse. It was hard to believe only a week ago he'd come to church with her. She'd secretly hoped he would show up today. But after the way she treated him, he'd probably stay clear of her. Who could blame him? She really messed things up. Not her finest hour. But she couldn't change it, so now she had to live with her actions.

At least he'd agreed he wouldn't sell the farm without offering it to her first. She might not end up with the guy, but it should be a consolation that she could keep her job and her home.

Thoughts of Jesse were interrupted as a large body stepped over Rose on their way to the empty seat. Her line of sight hit the back of a gray dress shirt while she shifted her knees out of the way. The man sat down just as the service started. She glanced over to give her new neighbor a friendly smile, only to be stunned to see Jesse.

The worship leader took the microphone and began welcoming the congregation.

With wide eyes, Rose stared dumbly at Jesse.

He smiled at her, wearing that crooked grin of his that she loved.

Slowly, she smiled back.

The congregation stood and started to sing. Together, Jesse and Rose joined in.

Rose couldn't stop smiling.

When the service ended, she nervously grabbed her purse and made small talk as the congregation shuffled outside. In the parking lot, Rose said a quick goodbye to Lolly and her parents.

Grammy hugged Rose, then pulled Jesse into a warm embrace. "I see you're still here," she said with a sparkle in her eyes. It wasn't a question this time, as though she expected him to leave any moment. Rather, she sounded happy to see him.

"Yes, ma'am," Jesse said, grinning.

"I'm no fool. I can see what's going on. All I have to say is, don't you hurt my Rose again."

"No, ma'am. I won't."

Rose couldn't believe her grandmother just said that. She bit her lip and looked away, pretending she hadn't witnessed the exchange.

Grammy left, and finally they were alone. There was so much Rose wanted to say, but she didn't know how to start.

"I'm surprised you came today," she said at last.

"Are you? Good. I wanted to surprise you."

"You did? Even after the way I behaved the other day at the firehouse?"

"What? That? It was nothing. I told you to forget about it."

They reached her car, and Rose turned to face him. "It was something, and I'm mortified I behaved that way. I'm sorry. I hope you'll forgive me."

"I guess you're not letting it go. Believe it or not, I understand why you were upset. I'm sure I looked pretty guilty when the investor stopped by the farm. Let's forget it ever happened."

"I'd like that." Relief filled her after agonizing over her blunder all week. Even though his text said he'd forgiven her, it was different talking to someone in person.

"And I have a confession," Jesse added. "I have a real surprise for you,"

He seemed like he was bursting to tell her something. His eyes sparkled with amusement, and he rubbed his hands together like he couldn't wait. He suddenly looked ten years younger, like the playful teenager he once was.

"What's the surprise?" Rose's heart fluttered as her own inner teen went giddy.

"It's waiting back at the farm. I have to show it to you for you to understand."

She cocked her head to the side as she tried to think of what in the world it could be. "Okay, I'll play along. This better be good."

"It is. Trust me," he said as he started backing away toward his car. "Meet you back at the farm." He ran across the church parking lot to where he parked.

The fifteen-minute drive to the farm felt like an eternity. Rose couldn't remember the last time she'd had a surprise. Perhaps it was that first day Jesse showed up at the farm. She'd been shocked to look across the barn and meet the laughing eyes of his handsome face while she gave her farm animal class. At the time it wasn't a wanted surprise, but life, it seemed, had a way of doing that.

They turned into the Sunflower Farms drive, and

Rose followed Jesse's car up to the gift shop. It was early, and the place was still closed to visitors. Jesse walked over to her as she climbed out of her car and took her hand.

"Where are we going?"

"To your surprise."

He pulled her along, every now and then glancing back at her.

"I think you're taking me to the garden. Am I right?" she asked.

"I don't know. Guess you'll have to wait and see," he teased.

The suspense was killing her. At last he stopped in front of the garden. A new large wooden sign hung in the archway. It was beautifully painted with rose vines and read Rose's Garden.

Rose gasped. "It… It's lovely… When did you have time to put this up?"

A wide grin broke across his face. "Why do you think I was late for church?"

She shook her head. "But I don't understand. Why did you put it up?"

He turned toward her and gently squeezed both her hands.."This is a gesture to show my gratitude to you for everything you've done. This is in honor of your amazing rose garden, but more importantly it's in honor of you, Rose. You are the best part of Sunflower Farms. You've been running it for years, and it's better than ever. Forget me selling the farm. I've decided to keep it, and I want you to be my partner. It will be ours together."

"Jesse… I… I…don't know what to say," she stuttered, heart racing.

"Wait, I'm not done. It's more than the farm. I've been searching for something that I couldn't put my finger on. I thought it was my job, but now I have figured it out. My life isn't complete without you. Rose, I want you to be my partner in life. I loved you when I was eighteen, and after all this time, I've come to realize that has not changed. I still love you… If you'll forgive me for leaving and have me back, you'd make me the happiest man in the world."

Rose felt her eyes water as she absorbed every word. "I'm so happy you came back. I've never stopped loving you, either." She squeezed his hands for emphasis. "I understand now, you did what you did for me. It hurt, I won't lie. But like you knew it was time to forgive your dad, I realize it's time to forgive you for leaving me and to trust you again."

Jesse leaned down and kissed her, then pulled back. "We've wasted so many years, when we could have been happy together."

"I think that was part of the journey in order for us to appreciate what we have now. And to appreciate what we'll have for years to come."

Jesse kissed her again, then pulled her tightly into his arms. Butterflies flew in her stomach. She would remember this moment forever. It was funny how life was like that—when least expected, a person could be blessed with something greater than they ever imagined. Rose felt those blessings profoundly. She had everything she'd ever wanted: friends, family, this amazing farm, and now Jesse, an incredible man that she loved. He was the last piece of the puzzle to make her life complete. In that moment, Rose's heart felt like it could explode with happiness, and she said a silent thank you to God.

Epilogue

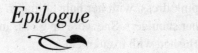

Two months later...

Jesse held the small box open. In it lay his grand-mother's engagement ring, passed down to his mother, and now it belonged to him. He'd found it while clean-ing out his parents' room that first week back on the farm. It was one of the few things he chose to keep because it was a family heirloom. Nervously, Jesse snapped the box closed and shoved it into the pocket of his pants.

Leaving his apartment in Jacksonville, Jesse made the one-hour drive to Sunflower Farms to pick up Rose for their date. One thing was for sure, he would not miss the long commute to the farm once they were married. He would move back to his childhood home…provided she said yes.

Jesse rubbed his sweaty palms on his pants as he drove. Why was he nervous? They loved each other. Why wouldn't she say *yes*? Still, he couldn't relax. It was such a big moment, and nothing was ever guaranteed.

Jesse drove down the farm's long driveway and parked below Rose's apartment. Anxious to see her, he took the stairs up two at a time, then knocked. He'd told her to dress up, that he wanted to take her somewhere nice for the evening. When she answered the door, she flashed him a brilliant smile. She looked radiant in a pink dress, with her hair falling in soft waves around her shoulders. She wore lip gloss, and her cheeks were flushed with excitement.

Her eyes grew wide when she saw him. "Wow. You look so handsome," she said. "You should wear a suit and tie more often."

"Thank you. And you look amazing," he complimented back.

Rose glanced down at her dress, "Oh, this old thing," she joked. Then daintily she lifted one foot, as if to model her shoe. "I even wore my new high heels."

"Very nice. Ready to go?"

"Yep. Let me grab my purse."

Jesse was keenly aware of the ring hidden in his pocket as they walked down the stairs holding hands. Did she notice his sweaty palm? If she did, she was polite enough not to say anything. He held the car door open for her.

"Thank you," she said, sliding gracefully into the car. Jesse rushed around to the other side and got in.

"Where are we going?" she asked as he started the engine.

"A nice little restaurant I found between here and Jacksonville."

"I'm surprised you wanted to dress up. I don't know what's gotten into you, Jesse Cooper, but I like it. I always knew you were a romantic at heart."

"Don't tell anybody," he teased, turning onto the country road.

After driving for five miles, he turned onto the highway. The evening sun was starting to set. They easily chatted as the miles slipped past them.

Finally, they reached their destination, a historic Victorian house that had been turned into a charming bistro. Jesse parked across the street in a small, crowded lot and they got out.

"This place is beautiful. How did you ever find it?" Rose asked.

"I heard a couple of the guys talking about it at the station and thought we could try it."

Jesse patted his pocket, to reassure himself the small ring box was still there. A zing of nervousness went through him.

They crossed the road and reached the front of the restaurant. "I can't wait to see their menu," Rose said. "I'm in the mood for..." Abruptly her words were cut off as she slipped on the first step and fell.

"Whoa!" Rose said, hitting the ground. It happened too fast for Jesse to catch her. Rose laughed it off as she collected herself and sat down on the bottom step. "I'm okay... Ooh, maybe not," she said, grabbing her ankle. "I should never have worn these heels."

Jesse crouched down and examined the injured ankle; it was already swelling. "I better take you to the emergency room. You may have broken it."

The nearest hospital was twenty-five minutes away in Jacksonville. They checked into the busy ER and waited hours to be seen. It was after ten o'clock when Rose was finally discharged with a badly sprained ankle. Jesse pushed her in a wheelchair toward the hospital exit.

"You think the restaurant is still open?" she asked, sounding hopeful.

"I called and they've already closed. Why? That pack of crackers we shared from the vending machine didn't fill you up?" he teased.

"Maybe as an appetizer, but that was hours ago. I'm starving."

"Yeah, me too."

After they left the hospital, Jesse spotted a fast-food joint from the highway and they stopped for burgers. Once they'd eaten, they had a good laugh at how the evening had turned out.

Finally turning in to Sunflower Farms, on impulse, he drove past Rose's apartment. The headlights lit a path through the grass ahead of them.

"Where are we going?" Rose asked.

"You'll see."

"Jesse Cooper, it's been a long night. Please don't play games with me."

"Rose McFarland, it's been a long night for me too. Just trust me."

Jesse took them to the field with the picnic tables. Stopping next to the table they had sat at the night of the barn dance, he helped Rose out of the car. She hobbled over, sat down on the wooden bench, and looked up at the dark sky. "It's such a clear night. There's millions of stars out tonight," she said in awe.

Jesse sat next to her and took a deep breath. He was

too nervous to stargaze. His heart raced in his chest, thinking about this important moment.

"This is nice. Thank you for bringing me out here." Rose said. "At least we can end the night on a good note."

Jesse stood up, reached in his pocket, and pulled out the little box he'd kept hidden all evening. When he knelt on one knee, in front of Rose, she gasped, covering her mouth with both hands.

"Jesse… What are you doing?" she asked breathlessly.

He flipped open the box so she could see the diamond ring.

"Rose, you are the love of my life. You bring me so much joy and I want to spend the rest of my life with you. Will you marry me?"

In the moonlight, Rose's eyes sparkled with unshed tears. "Yes. I'll marry you."

Jesse carefully took the ring out of the box and slipped it on Rose's finger. Then he stood, and pulled her up into his arms.

Now he was truly home.

* * * * *

Dear Reader,

Thank you for taking this journey with me to visit beautiful Sunflower Farms. I can picture row after row of large yellow blossoms swaying in the breeze, the perfect backdrop for Rose and Jesse's reunion.

As romance stories typically go, it was a rocky beginning. To quote Jesse, Rose was about as prickly as a porcupine, but who could blame her! I love how these two characters complement each other, and even after ten years, their love never faded. They were meant for one another.

I hope you noticed a common theme in this story. We may think we have our lives planned out, but often God has something else in store for us. It usually is nothing we can imagine but often so much better. I think this is something to remember in our own lives. I hope you've enjoyed this story and will look for more books from me in the future. Until then, keep reading!

Warm wishes,
Stacie